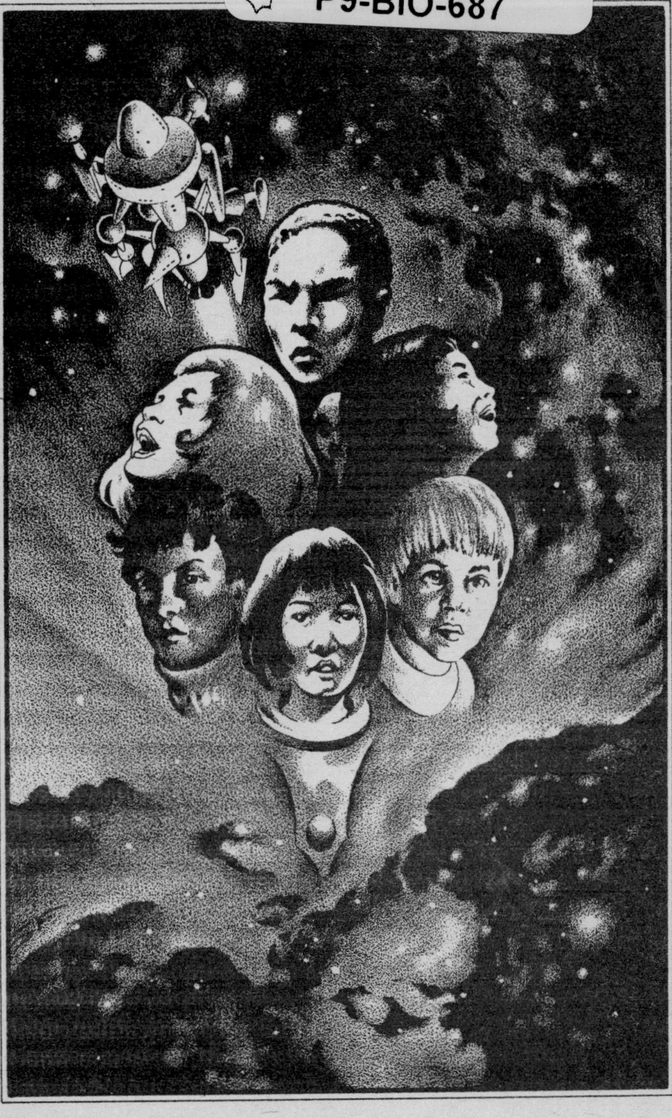

SURVEY SHIP

MARION ZIMMER BRADLEY

Illustrated by Steve Fabian

ACE SCIENCE FICTION BOOKS
NEW YORK

To Randall Garrett

SURVEY SHIP

An Ace Science Fiction Book / published by arrangement with
the author

PRINTING HISTORY
Ace Science Fiction edition / October 1980
Fourth printing / May 1986

ISBN: 0-441-79103-4

Ace Science Fiction Books are published by The Berkley Publishing Group,
200 Madison Avenue, New York, New York 10016.
PRINTED IN THE UNITED STATES OF AMERICA

PROLOGUE

How do you make a spaceman?

You start the same way that you start to make a chess master, a ballet dancer, a trapeze performer, or any other difficult and complex task demanding highly trained and concentrated skills, physical or mental; you start when the future professionals are too young to know whether that is what they want out of life, or not. Six is not too young.

United Nations Expeditionary Planetary Survey — UNEPS — starts every year with one hundred five-year-olds, discovered, in early testing, to be both mentally and physically superior.

There is neither elitism nor egalitarianism about the selection. The child of a World Controller or a United Nations Senator cannot be bought or bribed in; while any beggar from the gutters of Bombay or Chicago who notices that his child is exceptionally bright can bring him to a local center for testing. A hundred are chosen; after a year of preliminary, concentrated education, fifty of them are returned to their parents or guardians. They have, for the rest of their lives, no trouble at all in getting scholarships to whatever schools, colleges or graduate schools their parents choose for them, and they never have to worry about unemployment. Even the failures are superior.

Between six and seventeen, nine or ten more will be dropped because of accident, illness, or some previously undiagnosed physical problem; or sometimes, the intensive group living and training turns up a serious emotional instability. Once again, the dropouts have no trouble in finding highly paid, highly challenging work for the rest of their lives. At twelve, with the equivalent of an ordinary college degree, they begin to specialize, according to each one's particular talent; mathematical, verbal, mechanical, linguistic. Most of them have more than one talent. The mathematical genius with no talent for words, or the creative verbal child with no talent for sciences or mechanical skills, doesn't belong in this training; they usually get weeded out before seven.

By seventeen when they "graduate," the remaining forty or so are highly trained polymath specialists. It goes without saying that they are keyed up to fever pitch. On this calm December night in Australia, the Southern Cross blazing down from the zenith, the UNEPS Academy was darkened; but there was little sleep for any of the forty-three members of the class who would graduate tomorrow.

Tomorrow, at least thirty of them would fail; the final humiliating washout. Failure was a relative term, of course. Those who remained were assured of work, if not with UNEPS, with governments, space authorities, colonies, teaching, training, administration; the present President of the Academy, and the Secretary of the United Nations Space Authority, were both such "failures" and no one outside the Academy ever thought of them as failures at all. But for the lucky graduates — never more than ten, or fewer than four — there was a universe at their feet, if they could live to claim it.

For those graduates were given a UNEPS spaceship, a Survey Ship, with only one instruction for their final test:

Find us a planet. Find us a planet that UNEPS can colonize.

The lucky ones would be revered, worshipped, envied, and sometimes hated, especially by their classmates. Their nicknames, and their faces, would be known all over Earth within seconds of their selection. Their nicknames — but never their names, or the country of their origin. For, while the UNEPS Academy is in Australia, it is not subject to the current government of Australia; and the candidates, as soon as it is known that they will remain in UNEPS at the age of six, lose their names, and their nationalities, forever. They represent, not South Africa, or Mexico, or the United States, or England, but the United Nations — and Earth. They are, in the truest sense, Earthmen. No one knew, for instance, whether the present Secretary of the Space Authority was a black from Harlem, Haiti or Nigeria; whether the Academy President, who was known simply as Miri, her Academy nickname bestowed at seven, had been born in California or Hong Kong.

Every student's life, from his sixth year, is aimed at this goal; and all through their training, they know that only one in five — at the highest and most favorable odds — can possibly make it. Sometimes only one or two in a class can qualify. That year there will be no Ship. For each class is trained intensively as a unit — to function as a perfect team with the other members — and only with the members, of that one class. One surviving member of a non-qualifying class could not possibly be expected to merge with four or six or eight crewmen from a year other than his own.

And so on that last night, forty-three candidates lay awake, wondering, and dreading, and fearing, and there was little sleep. For at least thirty-three of them, these twelve years would end in failure. It didn't matter that their lives would be secure, filled with riches and rewards; it would still be failure. For their whole lives had been aimed toward sending them out on a Survey Ship.

There was a rumor floating around the school — nobody knew where it had started — that this year only six had been chosen.

Every one of the forty-three secretly believed that when that Survey Ship left Earth's orbit, he or she would be on it.

And at least forty-two of the forty-three secretly knew, in his or her despairing heart, that he, or she, would be left behind.

Every one of them had different ways of dealing with the tensions of that last night.

CHAPTER ONE

Peake and Jimson were together, as always, playing a Schubert *Nocturne* in the Music Room.

Earlier that day there had been the ceremony — broadcast by satellite all over the world — where the forty-three graduates passed on their torches to the forty-two remaining in the class who would graduate next year. Peake had been the leftover one, the one who had to stand with his class without a torch to hand to anybody, so that he had stood there, holding the torch awkwardly until it was unobtrusively taken and put out by one of the administrative personnel. That was the kind of person Peake was; tall, black and gangling, with rumpled hair and beaky features, his legs just a little too long for his uniform trousers; he was the one you always expected to trip over his own big feet, or spill the soup all over himself. Like a giraffe, he looked all-hung-together-anyhow, and awkward, and he was quiet and diffident as the result of catastrophic clumsiness in adolescence. But, like the giraffe, his loose parts somehow fitted; he never broke even the most delicate bit of laboratory equipment, and his huge, ham-sized, double-jointed fingers, now moving caressingly over the frets of the violin, had the precision of a surgeon — which is what he was.

Jimson, leaning over the keyboard, was very different; small, blonde, almost chubby — not overweight; the diet and exercise program of the Academy prevented that. But he had round features, and would never be tall; at seventeen he hadn't started shaving yet. His hands, though, looked even more muscular and competent than Peake's; they could span more than an octave. He had wanted to follow Peake into surgery or medicine, but they'd talked it over, at fifteen, and, knowing that two with the same specialty would never be chosen for the same crew, had decided to go different routes. Specialization was always the gamble; everybody in your own specialty was even more your rival than everyone else in the Academy.

Peake let his last note die, stood unmoving while Jimson played the final cadenza; ornate, cheerful, decorative. A good, unemotional choice for tonight, he thought, nothing that could bring on sentiment. Jimson rose, sighed a little, and watched Peake replace his violin in its case on the numbered rack. There were forty-three of them; everyone in the Academy played some instrument, all beginning together in Suzuki violin classes at five.

They walked together to their adjacent cubicles; and, as always, turned into the nearer one, which was Jimson's. The cubicles had already been stripped; traditionally, before the torch ceremony, all mementoes of the twelve years of training were thrown away, given away, or passed down to anyone in the next class who could use them. Ship members would take nothing from this life — except their own musical instruments — aboard the Ship; and gradually it had become customary for all members of a graduating class to part with their possessions as if each was going to the life of a Ship. Everyone would have to rebuild a new life anyway.

Jimson sprawled full-length on the cot; Peake crouched in the single chair, which was, like almost everything else, too small for him. At seven, David Akami had already been taller than anyone else in the class; he had been dubbed "Pike's Peak" which the years had gradually shortened to Peake.

"You've got surgery, deep-space navigation, geology, agronomy," Jimson repeated, obsessively, "I'm worried about that damned geology. I knew I ought to go into organic chemistry instead! And since all my other specialties are in the biological sciences — "

"They aren't going to get anybody on the crew who doesn't have at least one overlap with somebody else," Peake said gently, smiling at his friend, "It's a plus, if anything, that you can move outside the field of Life Sciences. You have linguistics and life support, too — I don't think the overlap matters all that much. Look, Jimmy," he went on, "We took a calculated risk and we have to be ready to stick by our decision. The two of us are right at the top of the class; nobody except Ching has a higher grade-point average — "

"But they don't always go by marks, and you know it," Jimson said, gloomily. "They take in compatibility, and personality, and there's something else too, that a couple — like us — might have trouble adjusting to living with others . . . that's why they want us not to make permanent commitments, on the chance that we'll be separated if one makes Ship and the other doesn't — "

"Hey Jimson, what's all this?" Peake interrupted with a grin. "We went all over that three years ago, and decided we had two choices; break up, or make us into such a great team they'd want both of us! At the worst, we'll both stay Earthside; at best, when that Survey

Ship pulls out, we'll both be on it, you in Life Support and me in Medic . . . ''

Jimson glared at his friend. "No, that's not the worst and you know it," he flung at him, "the worst would be that one goes and the other stays — and I ought to have known it years ago, damn it, why did I let you sell me a deal like that? A good Life-Support man who was a surgeon too — that would have been sure to get on the Ship!"

Peake looked at him in dismay; in twelve years in the Academy, each as the other's closest friend, they had never exchanged a harsh word. "Jimson, that's not fair; we decided it together. And anyhow, it would be too late to worry about it now. Are we going to spend our last night together fighting?"

"Yeah, you know it's going to be the last time, too, don't you?" Jimson flung at him with enormous bitterness, "You set it up just fine, didn't you, to eliminate at least one rival?"

Peake stared in consternation. But he had been intensively trained in group living and the avoidance of conflict. He unfolded his long legs, towering over the boy in the cot.

"I'm not going to quarrel with you, kid. I hoped we could spend tonight together — I think we both need it. But if you feel this way it wouldn't do either of us any good. Look, you'll feel better tomorrow, Reuben." The use of the private name, rather than the Academy-imposed nickname, was as much a caress as the dark fingers touching Reuben Jamison's light hair.

"Take it easy, kid. Save a seat in the auditorium for me if you get there first. Look," he added, eager to comfort, "whatever happens, the decision's made — one way or the other, nothing we can do is going to change it. Get some sleep, Reuben. It's settled, right or wrong, it's *done*. Relax."

Jimson flung after him, in sick misery, "Yeah, the decision's made, all right! You don't think they're going to take a pair of queers on their Survey Ship, do you?"

Peake, heartsick, closed the door.

The chapel was an afterthought in the Academy, built in, and still functioning in the style of, a time of agnosticism or atheism among the Establishment; teachers, and therefore almost all the students, were militant atheists. It had been built to appease a small pressure group who had been very vocal about the need for it, but there was no longer, even on paper, an official UNEPS chaplain. The chapel was used, now and then, for concerts of chamber music, and one of the Recreation Officers numbered, far down on the list of his purely nominal duties, that of chaplain and counselor.

Ravi sat there now, cross-legged, silent, breathing in and out almost imperceptibly. Small, dark-skinned, with sharply handsome features, he had been given his nickname because of a chance resemblance to a legendary musician from his own country of origin. Now, deep in meditation, for a time surface thoughts played back and forth across his mind.

It is done. They have made the choice. It is too late for wish or regret. In his heart Ravi was not sure he wished to be sent away from Earth, although his only memories of his world, outside the clean mathematical world of the Academy, were fragmentary; burning heat, blistering sky or torrential stinking rains, the festering sores of beggars crowding, which sometimes haunted him in uneasy nightmares. So that he wondered, sometimes, with something he was too well-trained to identify properly as *guilt*; why am I here, clean, fed, pampered, and they dying outside there? Images remained in his mind; his father, cross-legged on the ground before a silk-weaving loom; crowded streets, women still clad in saris and veils; but all of it had gone, except for these scattered, fading dreams.

Ravi had taken up meditation without any real purpose; many cadets tried it, as a method of relaxation, a simple cure for insomnia. To his own surprise, he had found that it fitted some small and formerly inaccessible corner of his own psyche, filled a need, scratched an itch he had never known that he possessed. Ravi had been trained as a scientist, not a mystic; he found himself uncomfortable, even while he did it, with the obsessive study he had taken up, of his own roots, of the culture of his native country — not forbidden, never that, but certainly never encouraged. He knew, intellectually, that he belonged to UNEPS, not to his own country. He knew, too, that if he had revealed any trace of his questionings and his inner search, he would have been laughed out of the Academy. And now he wrestled with a question he had not had enough training to regard as spiritual.

I am expected to regard God as superstition and mathematics as ultimate reality. Yet I feel, I know, God as ultimate reality and mathematics as one of His choicer games and methods of revealing Himself. I want to learn more about that, and how can I ever know the things I need to know, if I am sent into the greater vastnesses of outer space with no one except my crewmates? I have heard there will be only five of them, and they are even more ignorant of these realities than I am.

Am I being exiled from God in being exiled from the planet of man, His creation?

He let his consciousness drift in meditation, until his mind narrowed itself to a single point of awareness; somewhere, detached from himself, he wondered if

perhaps outer space was like that, a greatness beyond comprehension . . . like God?

God exists; I must simply trust in what is necessary for me. If God created the Universe, then surely he is everywhere in it, in the space between the stars . . . as much as here in my mind.

Fontana, small and dark and delicately made, with sleek dark hair and thick freckles, was in bed with Huff. They had been exploring each other's bodies with curiosity and good-natured affection for more than a year now, in their leisure moments; but both were conscious of the admonition against pairings or permanent commitments, and both had been seen, often enough, with others.

Now, lying at ease in the afterglow, she smiled at him, a pixie smile, and said, "I'm going to miss you, Huff. I'm going to miss *this* — " and she touched him, playfully. He chuckled.

"Sure of yourself, aren't you, girl? Well, I don't blame you; you're at the top of the class, you're sure to be on the crew."

Fontana smiled and shook her head. "Not sure at all. Only whatever happens, we're going to be separated. It's scary, Huff, they blend us together so well, teach us to care about each other, up to a point, and then, after graduation, no two of us are ever likely to work together again. Maybe ten of us — six this year, I heard somewhere — will stay together on the Ship. The rest of us — well, scattered all over the universe. But you're just as likely to make Ship as I am. You're a good navigator — "

"Not half as good as Ravi."

"And you're skilled in linguistics — "

"Jimson and Janet and Mei Mei and Smitty are all

better than I am."

Fontana shook her head. "No *way* they're going to take Jimson. Peake is sure to be chosen, and they won't take any couple. No more than they'd take Dolly and Smitty — didn't you hear Dolly almost got thrown out because she had been careless and they thought she was pregnant? I'm pretty sure about Peake and Ravi. And Ching."

"Ching," Huff said with a groan. "Damn human computer! I thought they made the choices for compatibility too — how are they going to square it to take along Ching? Nobody likes her!"

"I wouldn't say that," Fontana said, with scrupulous fairness. "Huff, are you still prejudiced, just because she's a G-N?"

"That's an insult," Huff said, frowning. "Do you really think I'd keep that kind of superstitious prejudice? Maybe outside UNEPS, they think the G-Ns aren't human, but, damn it, I *know* Ching's human. I've seen her bleed, I've seen her cry when she was hurt. Logically, I know the only difference between Ching and the rest of us is that somebody tinkered with her mother's ovaries about ten months before she was born, and as a result, she has perfect genes for high IQ, musical talent, superior muscular tone, slow heartbeat, efficient hemoglobin use, perfect inner ear channels, and so forth."

"And yet — " Fontana said.

"And yet. I'm *human*. I resent the G-Ns. Who wouldn't? The G-Ns are phasing out the human students in the Academy. In the class below us, there are already twenty G-Ns; humans can't compete with them. G-N cadets will make us all obsolete some day."

"Don't be silly," Fontana said with some heat. "The G-Ns are just as human as we are. They're the *best* of humanity, that's all. Would you prefer to deny humanity the best, just to preserve some of the worst? Is there any moral *rightness* to a person being born tone deaf or with hemophilia or sickle-cell anemia? By *that* reasoning, you'd think women had some god-given right to have a Mongoloid child, or one with something horrible like Tay-Sachs disease!"

"But they all act so superior! The ones in next year's class aren't so bad. But Ching was the first, and she knows it, and I can't stand that damn *superiority* of hers!"

Fontana said, "That's not fair. Put yourself in her place, Huff. She knows she's different; she *is* superior. Yet she hasn't made herself hated. All of us here have IQs somewhere between 150 and 185. Ching's is so far over 200 that they can't even measure it, because there's no one who could make up a test. She's — careful. Not that anyone here would hate her — anyone who's capable of real hate gets weeded out of the Academy a lot younger than this. Ching's not arrogant; she's diffident, that's all. She doesn't want to — to swing her weight. Understand?"

"No," Huff confessed, "but I don't expect to. When you decided to specialize in Psychology, you lost me. And," he added, hugging her suddenly, "I'm going to miss you, Fontana. Listen — " he said shyly, "do you know I don't even know your name?"

"You never asked," Fontana said, touching his cheek. "I know yours, because I worked one year with the Rosters. You're Jurgen Hoffmeister, and I think Huff is a *lot* better as a name. The *names* people out there give to their kids!"

"It's funny," Huff said softly, "I keep forgetting, but sometimes, when I'm half asleep, I hear my mother saying my name. Jurgen. I called her *Mutti* or *Mutterl*.

I never speak anything but English, here. But when I'm asleep I remember."

"I know," Fontana whispered, "I don't remember my mother. I don't think I had one. But I remember I had a sister. She was bigger than I was. Her name was Consuelo. I wonder if she's still alive? I wish sometimes they'd let us know. But she would think of me as *Maria*, and wonder who *Fontana* was. She'll — if I'm chosen for the Ship — she'll see me and never know that I'm her sister."

"I think that's why they give us nicknames," Huff murmured, "so that every mother, or father, can look at us and wonder, is that my son, or daughter, is that my Jurgen, my Maria? And never be sure, but always think it *could* be."

Fontana rolled over and buried her head in his shoulder. She said roughly, "Hey, you're not so bad a psychologist yourself, at that. Cut it out before I start to cry."

"Sure," he agreed, and began fondling her again. But she was crying, and so was he.

Before nightfall, Teague had requested permission to leave the Academy grounds, and had driven his flitter up to the Observatory. The official who gave it had stared at the chunky, freckled lad in sloppy fatigue uniform, but he had signed the permission slip; there was no reason not to. Except for class hours, the students had unrestricted freedom. Teague had explained that his final examinations, and the ceremony earlier that day, had interfered with some photographic studies he had made of a transit of Venus last week, and he wanted to examine them carefully before leaving.

In the Observatory darkroom he worked away happily for many hours, unnoticed, until one of the night

watchmen — all of whom knew him, for he spent a substantial part of his time there — asked, "Isn't it your class that's graduating tomorrow?"

And then James MacTeague had blinked, grinned, and thought to himself; so *that's* why they looked at me so funny when I signed out. Our last night, and all that. It *is* tomorrow, isn't it?

But then the buzz on the developer sounded, and he went back to his slides. He didn't have much time to finish up.

Moira was in the jacuzzi, neck-deep in hot water, the bubbling jets streaming against her naked body, her red hair streaming on the surface. There were eight or ten other cadets in the jacuzzi with her, crowded so close that the water spilled out on the fiberglas deck; most of them male, and each convinced that he was *the* one Moira wanted there.

Not that Moira was a tease; it was only high spirits and good nature. She had done the usual amount of sexual experimentation, but never to the point where it interfered with her standing in her classes — right at the top, just below Ravi, Peake and Ching, who were the intellectual standouts in her year, and had been so since they were nine years old — and she had left no broken hearts in the wake of her good-natured sexiness.

She moved sensuously in the tub, revelling in the feel of the bubbling hot water against her long limbs. Next to her, Scotty said, "Has your ESP told you anything about which of us is going to be on the crew, Moira?"

She chuckled. "No luck there, Scotty. Too bad. I don't have even a clue; it only kicks in when there's a real emergency, which is why they could never manage to test it in laboratory conditions. They can't *fake* an emergency, because I *know* — and as long as there's no real danger, the ESP just *sits* there, and isn't the least good to me! It doesn't even warn me ahead of time if I'm going to break a cello string in the middle of a quartet," she added, with a rueful headshake. "It's only for *real* disasters."

"I'd think a Wild Talent like that would make you a top choice for crew," Mei Mei, the only other woman in the tub, said, and Moira shook her head.

"Too unreliable. And they think it's phasing out as I get older, anyhow. More likely they'll try cloning me, and see if it's genetic or reproducible." Moira frowned, remembering the time she had absolutely refused, for no reason she could identify, to go on a piece of playground equipment. She had been given a severe lecture on obedience and antisocial behavior by the playground director, who had been killed, five minutes later, when the equipment collapsed under five children, under Moira's horrified eyes.

Would that special talent be a handicap or a benefit on a Survey Ship? Moira didn't know. Tuning her ears to the sound of the jacuzzi, amusing herself by locating from that soft sound the hidden flaw in the machinery which would, if not fixed, put the pump out of commission within four or five days, she reminded herself to tell the maintenance man before she left the pool area. *That* was the talent that would win her a place on the Ship, if she did win a place, she told herself. The knowledge, so deep-rooted that it was almost instinctive, of how machines worked, and what could interfere with the working. Nobody had noticed the flaw in the sound of the pump, which increasingly grated on her ears like a false note in a Haydn quartet. The pump was like an apparently healthy man with a small, asthmatic rasp which ought to warn a doctor of incipient emphysema, but seldom did.

Scotty was murmuring to her, caressing her freckled breast under the hot water, but she pushed him impatiently away.

"Later, Scotty. Something's wrong with the pump, I've got to go and tell the janitor."

"It sounds fine to me," Mei Mei said. "Are you having psychic flashes again, Moira?"

"No, no," Moira said, impatiently. "Can't you *hear* it?" Machines, she thought, climbing wet and dripping out of the jacuzzi and draping a huge towel about her body, had to be perfect. They were so much more reliable than human talents. She listened, frowning, to the almost-imperceptible sound, tilting her head, gritting her teeth. *Poor old fellow,* she whispered to the laboring machinery, *just take it easy, we'll have you fixed up and comfortable pretty soon, I'll make sure they take good care of you.*

And in her solitary cubicle in the dormitory where the other students, alone or together, tried to forget tomorrow and the impending finality of the choices, the small, slight, dark-haired girl who had been dubbed "Ching" in her first week in the Academy, stood brushing her teeth before the mirror. The teeth were perfect — any predisposition toward dental or gum disease had been eliminated from her altered genetic makeup. Academy nutrition and conscientious brushing kept them that way.

She had the Oriental eye-fold; the insemination donor who had "fathered" her, she had been told, was a Japanese architect. But her face was too much a racial blend to have any other distinguishing characteristics. Even a touch of ugliness, she thought, would have made her more interesting. But, like all G-Ns — Genetically

ENgineered Superiors — her face was boringly average
and ordinary. She wondered if the scientists who had
created the G-Ns had done it that way so that there
would not be one more thing for the ordinary, genetically mixed humans to envy; great beauty would have
set them even further apart from everyone else.

Tonight she had kept to the exact routine she had
known all her life; she had put on a tape of one of her
favorite violin sonatas, later practiced a half hour on
the viola as she had every night since her fifth year,
and now, her teeth brushed and tingling with cleanli-
ness, she showered and went peacefully to bed, wondering how showers and other hygienic maneuvers
would be managed in the low gravity of a Ship. Alone
among her classmates, she knew she would be chosen.
The experiment which had created the G-Ns was an
unqualified success; in the class below Ching, there
were twenty of them; two classes below her, there were
forty, and not one had dropped out due to illness or
physical or mental incompetence. The other G-N in
Ching's class, the one that would graduate tomorrow,
had left them on her fifteenth birthday; some unsus-
pected randomness in the engineered musical talent
had given her such a soprano voice as was heard only
once or twice in a generation, and she had left, with
the blessing of the Academy, to pursue a concert career.
Ching thought, a little wistfully, of Zora — who had
been given back her own name, Suzanne Hayley, and
her own nationality, which was Canadian. She, Ching,
would never be anything but Ching, of the UNEPS
Academy. No name, no country, only a Ship, and fame
she would not be able to enjoy. Zora had been allowed
to follow her own choice and her own destiny.

But the G-Ns were certainly the wave of the future;
some day, no doubt, the G-Ns would be the staff of all

the Survey Ships. Ching had no doubt that next year's
class would be the full Ship complement of ten, instead
of leaving it to competitiveness. And she, Ching, had
been chosen to be the first to test the sufficiency of
G-Ns, and that ought to be enough.

She was an experiment; she had been lonely, having
no real peers. And no real friends, either, she thought
with a touch of cynicism. They tolerated her, because
there was no room in the Academy for anyone who
could not get along with all kinds, and any dislike or
unfairness shown to Ching would have damaged that
person's career more than Ching's. But she sometimes
envied Moira's hordes of admirers and her easy sex-
uality, even admired the close tenderness of Peake and
Jimson while she recognized its unwisdom. There was
no one *she* had ever cared for that much, and no one
who had cared so much for her; she supposed, a little
wryly, that she was the only virgin in her class.

It was worse, she supposed, than being a member of
a racial minority in the old days. But she *was* different,
and there was no point in resenting it. Ching turned
on her side, and within minutes was peacefully asleep.

CHAPTER TWO

The Ship had been constructed in free orbit, free of the limitations of gravity — on Earth it would have weighed so many tons that the fuel costs of lifting and moving would have been multiplied exponentially. The hull had been constructed from metal refined and manufactured within a Lunar Dome, and the machinery assembled and tested there. The Ship had a name; for political reasons — there were still some of those on Earth — she had been called after a little-known general in the Space Service a hundred years ago. But not one of the crew ever called her, or were ever to call her, anything except The Ship. Anyone who needed to refer to this particular Ship, as distinguished from others, would have had to look up the name in an official register, by the year.

The six members of the crew had their first sight of the Ship from the observation deck of the Lunar shuttle. Only Moira and Teague, both of whom had specialized in the drive units and had helped, with the others in their class who had studied space engineering, to assemble her, had ever seen her before. Ching had worked with identical computers, but had never seen this particular one. She picked out the small, spherical computer module. Peake and Ravi had studied deep-space navigation on simulators and mockups. As for Fontana, she had never been in free-fall, except in the training centrifuge, and brief trips in free-fall transit rockets; she spent the trip out trying to conquer her faint queasiness.

From space the Ship looked something like a collection of paper sculptures, strung together in a cluster anyhow, without need for the high-speed streamlining of Earth or gravity, and without any kind of linear organization. There would be sufficient gravity to make the crew comfortable and keep them fit — the DeMag gravitators were the only thing which had made deep-space voyages practicable from a human biological standpoint. But gravity could be sharply localized for the crew's comfort in a given spot or area; there was no need to orient the Ship on any given axis. Inside, the arrangements made sense; but from outside it looked chaotic. Teague thought the Ship looked like a collection of helium balloons which had somehow drifted together — balloons which just happened to be spherical, cubical, octahedral, or conical.

Moira was wondering what it would look like from the outside when the enormous sheets of thin mylar, the light-sails which operated on solar pressure, were spread out around the conglomeration of shapes. Peake thought, sadly, that Jimson had never seen the Ship — then revised that thought. Jimson was probably seeing it right now, or at least, he had seen it this morning from the space station; he had probably had a good look at it from the Lunar Shuttle, too. Jimson had been assigned as an administrative assistant on the space station, and would probably be in charge of it, a few years from now.

I wonder if he feels like Moses, looking from afar at the Promised Land?

Jimson hadn't spoken to Peake when the announcements were made. Not once.

And then the Shuttle was drawing up alongship, and they were going through the motions of getting into pressure suits — second nature now, after years of drill on it — and decanting through the airlock. Only minutes later, they were in the DeMagged main cabin, watching the airlock close and the Lunar Shuttle pull away, and Peake realized that there was no one to give the order, this time, to get out of pressure suits. So he checked the pressure of the cabin, shrugged, and unfastened his own helmet, hanging it meticulously in the rack.

Six of us, Moira thought, alone with the Ship which has been our goal, our summit, our daydream for the best part of twelve years. *Is that all there is to it?* They had all been expecting some more formality than this. But what more could there be? They were the graduates, they had been given the final sink-or-swim test. If they had not been capable of functioning on their own, without further instruction, they would be now among the failures, serving apprenticeships on space stations, satellites, governing the Earth colonies some day — but they were the independent ones. This Ship gave them the freedom of the universe, and they had to prove themselves in it. They would evolve their own procedures, they would make themselves into a crew — or they would not; it was just as simple, and as enormous, as that.

Suddenly she was frightened, and, looking around at her five shipmates, she was sure they were frightened too. ESP? she wondered, and thought; no; just common sense. If we weren't scared, we wouldn't be as bright as we have to be, just to have come this far.

"Look," said Peake, "there is your cello, Moira. And

my violin.''

Ching looked at her viola, in its case. These were the
only really personal articles they would retain from
Earth and the life that was past. She said into the lengthening silence, ''Well, here we all are. What do we do
first?''

''I was taught,'' Teague said dryly, ''that the first thing
you do on any Ship is to check the Life-Support system,
and I imagine that's my job — I don't think there's anyone else here who specialized in Life-Support systems.''

''My second specialty,'' Fontana said. ''I suppose I'll
be your standby.''

''Well — shall I go and do it?'' Teague looked around,
then realized there was no one to tell him to do it or
not to do it. He said ''Right. As I remember from the
plan, the main Life-Support system should be through
the door there — airlock — sphincter — whatever you
call it.'' He turned toward it. Peake said, ''We might as
well all go. We'll have to learn our way around,'' and
followed Teague and Fontana. The others came crowding after.

As Teague thrust himself through the dilating
sphincter, he experienced a sudden, violent shift of
orientation. His feet had been ''down''; suddenly he
was head-down, his feet somehow ''over his head.''
Even though he knew instantly what had happened,
that he had moved from a DeMag gravitator located
toward the floor of the main cabin, into a DeMag field
located at the other apex of the corridor he had entered,
it took him a moment to get his flailing feet ''down.''
Peake actually tumbled and fell. Moira did an athlete's
flip and came up standing. And then, to all of them,
''down'' was where it was, and they looked back at the
crazy, somehow disoriented airlock which seemed to

be in the "ceiling" of the present room.

"Wow," Teague muttered, "that's going to take some getting used to!"

"The Life-Support stuff looks familiar, anyhow," Fontana said, and they went toward it. "All new and shiny, anyhow."

"Do you suppose we'll ever get used to it, after that battered old stuff we learned on at the Academy?" Teague asked. "They sure didn't skimp on shiny new state-of-the-art stuff, did they?"

Fontana was studying the air-supply mechanisms. "It's like all new systems; has to be tested and run in, checked out for bugs," she said, "and I'm not happy with that mixture of inert gases."

"You won't find any bugs in it, any more than in the drives," Moira said. "I installed most of it myself." Her voice was defensive, and Fontana shrugged, not willing to pursue the matter.

"Time will tell, I guess. Look, they have touch-set monitors, and the flow system is backed up there, so that we can monitor oxygen, air, and DeMags in every part of the Ship on this visual tell-tale —"

Ching peered over her shoulder. "Does that mean you can see into every room and watch what we're doing?"

"Hell no," Teague replied, his hands already moving on the air-system console, "who needs to? But we can use sensors to find out how much air and oxygen there is in any sector; if one of us should be unconscious, we can locate whoever's missing, or if there's air-loss anywhere." He was running his hands over protein synthesizers. "Looks all right, and there's enough raw material in the converters that with molecular-fusion techniques we can synthesize everything we're likely to need for the next, I should roughly say, twenty-nine

years; after which time we find a sun with something
like the chemical composition of our own, and catch
ourselves a small asteroid or two for the next eighty or
ninety. That's assuming that we recycle clothing and
water, but not figuring in body-waste recycling."

"I want to see the drives," Moira said. "I put them
in; but I want to see them in their place in the Ship."

Teague smiled at her and touched the console again.
"Looks like we have a considerable way to go, to get
there; the drive chamber's at the far end of this walk-
way —" he pointed, "furthest from the living quarters.
Navigation and computer areas are closer."

Another of the dizzying gravity-reversals brought
them down — or, at least, "down" — to another module, this one spherical, with seats and many controls.
"You'll drive the Ship from here anyway, Moira,"
Peake pointed out, indicating the console for manip-
ulation of the light-pressure sails.

She said, "I want to see the hardware itself. See how
it looks *in situ*." Nevertheless, she slid gracefully into
the contour seat, her hands hovering over, but not
touching the console.

"Where are we going? Which way?"

Peake realized, with shock, that nobody knew. "I
guess it depends on who's the chief navigator," he said.
"It was my second specialty, so I suppose I'll be navigator's assistant."

Ravi looked up at him, eyes raised in a quizzical grin.
"I thought you'd be first navigator. My second specialty
was navigation, too. What do we do — toss a coin for
it?"

Peake looked around the spherical chamber. One half
of it was an opaqued wall of glass looking out on the
universe. The DeMag was turned high enough so that
they could sit at their seats, without floating away in

free-fall. Before him a multitude of blinking lights, coded yellow, red, green, blue, flashed quietly, and he had the sensation that they were waiting. Moira touched a control, and the glass wall which reflected the blinking lights, suddenly became clear. In spite of the DeMag units giving them an "up" and "down" orientation, they all gasped and clutched at the nearest support; outside was only the vastness of space, white with stars, so thick that there was no sign of constellations. They could have read small print by that light. Against the blaze of stars Peake could still see the faint reflections of blue, red, yellow, green control lights, imposing their own order on the chaos outside.

Ravi was still looking at him expectantly. Ching said, "Which one of you had the highest grades in navigation?"

"Not enough difference to matter, over three years," Peake said, "and I'm a doctor, not a navigator. Does one of us have to be above the other? I'd rather share navigation on a time basis, not a rank basis — we're a fairly healthy crew or we wouldn't be here."

Ravi shrugged. "Okay; I'll toss you for day or night watch, if you want to do it that way, or until we see it isn't working. The one whose shift it is makes any necessary decision. Fair enough?"

"I don't think that makes much sense," Ching said. "There has to be one person with the responsibility for decisions — the commander, captain, whatever. I thought chief navigator was usually in that spot. Who's going to be making major decisions?"

"I don't think it ought to be *who*, but *how*," Moira said, swinging the seat around to face them. "Consensus decisions, I'd say, for anything major. Small decisions, whoever's running the special machinery involved."

Ching said, "I don't agree. Someone has to decide —"

"I had more than enough of structured decisions in the Academy," Peake said. "I'm ready to try sharing decisions on a group basis. If that doesn't work, there'll be time enough to try something else."

Ching shook her head. She said, "We could come up against something serious, so serious there wouldn't be time for a consensus, and there ought to be one person in charge —"

"What's your specialty, Ching?" Fontana asked with a smile, "group dynamics and sociology?"

Ching said stiffly, "I wouldn't dignify that by the name of a science at all. I am a computer technician and biochemist, with meteorology and oceanography as planet-based specialties. But as part of this group I do feel I have a vested interest in designating competent leadership for making decisions."

"There's a lot of logic to that," Fontana said, reflecting that it was probably the first time she had agreed with anything Ching said, "but I think we should check out the rest of the Ship before we start arguing about it. It looks as if you will be in charge of the computer, Ching. It's through there — shall we take a look at it? Though the central computer console seems to be in here, with navigation and drive consoles —"

Ching smiled. She slid into the seat past Moira's, and it seemed to Fontana that the small, rigid body relaxed slightly as she looked at the main computer console. Then she looked up, with a faint, challenging stance.

"Anyone else?"

Silence. Ching demanded, "Nobody else at all? Isn't there anyone with even a third or fourth in computer technology?"

Teague said, "Looks like it's all yours, Ching."

She looked stricken.

"That doesn't make sense! I'd hoped for Chris, or Mei Mei, or Fly — somebody with some computer sense — but I can't *believe* they sent us out without a single computer technician except me!"

"Obviously," said Peake, "they decided that with you, they didn't need anyone else."

Ching gave him an angry, suspicious glare. "Are you trying to be funny?"

"Not at all," Peake said. "Why would they need two computer experts on one ship? You'll have it all to yourself."

Ching protested, "But they *always* have a backup technician — " and she sounded almost frightened. Nevertheless, Fontana thought, as Ching moved and settled deeper into the seat, there was a touch of satisfaction, too.

Ching must know she's not really liked; maybe it will give her the kind of confidence she needs, to know she's really indispensable.

"It's not all that bad," Moira protested, "the Ship's drive is a computer, tied into the main one; and I know how to handle *that*."

"And for all your comments about psychology and sociology not being exact sciences," Fontana added, "I know how to get linguistics analysis from a computer — including yours."

"Not to mention," Ravi said, "that navigation and astronomy both demand computer access and skill. I don't think there's any one of us, Ching, who doesn't know how to use a computer. Probably that's why they had only one specialist —"

"But what if there's trouble? If I'm the only one who knows enough about the hardware —"

Peake said, "You'll have to choose one of us and

teach him, or her, how to take the thing apart in case of emergency. We're going to have a lot of time with nothing much to do, once we're out of the Solar System, and before we reach the nearest stars and star-colonies. We'll be navigating our way out of the Solar System, but at standard acceleration that won't take more than a few days —"

"Not that long," Ching said, and began to touch buttons on the console, but Ravi said, "twelve days, four hours, nine minutes, and a few seconds."

Ching swung her chair around, incredulous. Fontana thought she looked angry. "What do you —"

Peake said, "I'd forgotten. You're the one they call the human computer, Ravi."

He shrugged, looking almost as uncomfortable as Ching. "It's one of the commoner Wild Talents. I'm not the only lightning calculator in the Academy."

Ching looked at her console, where the same thing was printed out. She said, her face twisting slightly, "I guess if the computer gets out of order we can use you, then, can't we?"

"Take it easy, Ching," Moira said, soothingly, but the edge of mockery was clearly perceptible in her voice. "I don't think Ravi really meant to come between you and your best friend, did you, Ravi?"

"By no means," Ravi said, ignoring mockery and soothing alike. "Your talents will be needed for anything serious, Ching — that was a purely automatic arithmetical calculation. We must find out where we are going, and when, and how. Do we get orders?"

Peake said, quietly, "I think, when they gave us the Ship, we were given the only orders they were going to give us. All they care about is whether we find them a habitable planet. Ching, you have the resources of the computer, you know where planets have already been

discovered and surveyed for colonization. Teague, you
and Ravi can find out how far away they are and how
to reach them, and Ravi and I, as navigators, can set a
course so that Moira can take us there. Fontana and I
will, presumably, keep us alive and healthy while we're
en route there. And thank whatever Gods you believe
in that there are six of us. Suppose only four of us had
qualified, and we had to run a ship *that* way?"

There was a brief, stunned silence. Moira said, into
it, "I want to check the drives, and I suppose Ching
wants to look at the computer hardware."

Ching said, "We can't all go in there; I'll survey it
from outside. Computers are temperamental things,
and too many strange bodies around them can make
them do peculiar things. Nobody goes in there except
under absolute necessity; and then, wearing anti-elec-
trostatic garments, and special shoes. I'll be running it
from here."

"The drives are ready to go," Moira said. Peake,
watching her, thought she touched the controls of the
drive mechanism as if they had been the frets of her
cello — or the body of a lover. "So when do we leave?"

"As far as I know," Peake said, "it's up to us. When
we're ready, we go — and that's all there is to it."

And the six members of the crew looked at one another, stunned, realizing that after twelve years of rigid
structure, that really was all there was to it. No one
would give them orders. No one would tell them where
to go, or what to do.

Fontana looked out through the huge window with
the blaze of billions of stars, the tiny blinking lights of
the control panels reflecting, small and somehow lost,
against the hugeness of the unknown Galaxy; as if in
answer to the sudden terror of it, Ching touched something that closed them in again, the window opaque,

so that they were again sealed in the control cabin with only the winking lights and their reflections.

"There's no hurry," Fontana said, and her voice was shaking, so that she clung to a bulkhead. "Let's go back to the main cabin, and look over our living quarters, and find out who's going to sleep where. And have something to eat."

CHAPTER THREE

There was a window in the main cabin, but it was one of reasonable proportions, not a wall of glass that opened naked on the empty universe of Chaos; and as they watched, the familiar form of the space station, revolving slowly end-over-end (from their point of view) and trailing its little cone of shadow, came into view, trundled majestically across their window, and disappeared again. Against its known contours, the six could put themselves into human perspective again.

Fontana, trained to self-understanding because of her specialization in psychology, realized that they had all suffered their first attack of a kind of culture shock; the transfer from the orderly and rigid world of the Academy into the knowledge of a universe literally at their feet. Deliberately, searching for another touch of the familiar and banal, she went to the food console, and dialed herself a snack and a cold fruit drink.

"They stocked us with three months' supply of ready food; after that, we'll have to start synthesizing proteins and carbohydrate equivalents," she said. "We might as well enjoy it while we have it. With all these heavy scientific specialties on the crew, I don't suppose there's anyone who can cook?"

"I can," Ching said, "but I don't want to be stuck to

do it all the time."

"I think once a day would be enough for anyone to do it," Moira said. "Surely we can all fix our own breakfasts and lunches — even if we're not all on different schedules. I can cook, too — I'll do it once in a while."

"So what do we do? Set up a roster?"

Moira said, "I think we'd all get fed up with too much togetherness. Surely one meal a day together would be enough, if not too much?"

Ravi said, "I think we should share as many mealtimes as possible, considering duty rosters. We are the only human contacts any of us is going to have, for a long, long time; I think we should retain a — a base of closeness. To keep in touch. Make ourselves into a family."

"I'd go stir-crazy," Ching said. "I'd say, why not let everybody fix their own meals unless they really crave company; have dinner together once in ten days or so."

Peake was staring at the window, watching the space station come into sight again and slowly roll across their field of vision. Was Jimson there? They were as cut off from one another as if they had been at opposite ends of the universe, separated by a slowly lengthening string which would eventually snap and part them irrevocably. Already it was irrevocable. He felt desperately alone, surrounded by these five strangers. Yet not wholly strangers, either; he had known them all since kindergarten, many of them had been his friends until, in the last two or three years, he had focused all his attention and awareness on Jimson. Could they be his friends again? He said, "I think it would be a good idea to schedule one meal a day together. Not so often that we'd get claustrophobic, not so far apart that we'd get out of touch."

Teague said diffidently, "I wouldn't mind getting to-

gether once a day. Only I don't think it ought to be a
meal. Because if we get together once a day it's going
to turn into a — a kind of gripe session; we'll want to
get everything off our chests. And I hate to eat while
I'm arguing — or vice versa," he added with a grin.

"I think we ought to have a once-a-day conference,
whether it's a meal or not," Ching said. "Call it a gripe
session, brainstorming, business meeting, scientific
conference, or whatever. But we all ought to get together once a day."

"Is there any reason we have to keep a standard 24-
hour day and night?" Moira asked. "I tend to be a night
person, myself, and I'm never really awake before midnight. And I happen to know — because I roomed next
door to her for two years — that Ching's awake at the
crack of dawn, and is asleep by the time I'm beginning
to feel halfway human! Here we could have a round-
the-clock schedule not tied in to somebody else's idea
of when people ought to wake up and go to sleep!"

Peake said, "Biologically speaking — and speaking
as a medical man — I think we need circadian rhythms
maintained as long as we can possibly manage it. If
there's one thing I've learned about space medicine,
it's this: Earth man, *homo sapiens*, is firmly tied in to
the rhythms of his native planet's rotations. Biology is
destiny, at least to *that* extent. We *need* a 24-hour cycle,
give or take a little one way or the other. And while
we're on that subject, do all of you girls menstruate?"

"If you think that makes any difference —" Moira
began angrily, but Fontana interrupted. "Hold on,
Moira; the question is purely for practical reasons. Free-
fall — and we can hardly keep the whole ship De-
Magged to one gravity all the time — does peculiar
things to hormones, both male and female."

"That's right," Peake said, "and I was thinking we

could work out a duty roster which would allow any woman who's menstruating to work inside the De-magged areas for comfort. The question is medical, not sexist."

Fontana shrugged. "It's academic for me," she said. "I opted for hysterectomy when they offered it to all of us at fifteen. I knew that after a year in deep space there was a fifty-fifty chance I'd be sterile anyhow, so it seemed a lot of trouble for the next thirty years, for nothing. And it seemed a good idea to put it out of my power to have any second thoughts on the subject. I chose once and for all."

"I didn't," Moira said. "After reading up on both sides of the question, I decided I'd prefer having natural to synthetic hormones. But I'm not asking for special treatment."

Ching smiled, a little grimly. "I wasn't given the op-tion. I knew if I didn't make Ship, they'd want my genes. But I don't want special treatment; I think if any of us had severe menstrual problems, they'd take that into account before sending us into zero-gee work. I've always been boringly normal; if I have trouble, I might ask for a day off now and then, but I doubt I will. Let's leave it until the problem arises." She moved to the console, dialed herself a helping of some squishy semi-solid; Moira wondered if it was mashed potatoes or soft ice cream.

Teague said, "The cabins are in a circle in the next module; they're numbered one to six. Why not just take them in alphabetical order — Ching, Fontana, Moira, Peake, Ravi, and me in that order?"

Fontana giggled, biting into her ham sandwich — she supposed it was synthetic protein, but it tasted like a ham sandwich, so she decided to think of it as one. "That still separates women from men, three on a side!

Purely by the accidents of the alphabet!"

"I don't expect we'll be spending all that much time in the sleeping quarters," Moira said, "they make the cubicles at the Academy seem like auditoriums. One sleeping net and one shower with toilet per private cabin, and that's it."

"Wearing disposable clothing, that's about all we need," Ching said. "I notice they've each got separate DeMag units, though —"

"That's so you can read, study, or write without the books and papers floating away," Peake said, "and sleep at full gravity. And if you want to practice in private, your instrument will stay put . . . I assume you all know the mechanics of a violin depend on gravity, so you can get friction against the strings. The gym is set for one-half to two gravities, for physical training. I assume I don't have to warn you to work out at full gravity at least half the time, so your muscles won't atrophy."

"And speaking of music," Moira said, "I'd like to know if we have a complete string quartet. I play cello, and I know you play viola, Ching, because I've played with you. Ravi, you play the violin, don't you?"

"Only the way we all do. I haven't touched one since I was fourteen; I play the drums. Jazz drums, steel drums, and the Indian tabla. And somehow I think all I have here on the Ship is a small set of tabla — weight problem."

"Teague, you play —"

"Flute, wooden recorder, and several woodwinds. I could probably manage second violin sometimes. Peake's the best violinist we have on board."

Moira said, "I guess that makes you our concertmaster, then, Peake —"

He looked away and a spasm of pain crossed his face.

*That last day in the music room, his violin tucked
under his chin, Jimson's piano delicately interlocking
with his mind. . . .* He said thickly, "Look, let's leave
it, I'm not going to feel much like playing for a while.
Do you mind?"

"Yes, I do," Moira said, setting her chin. "You know
as well as I do why we were taught the violin, and
required to specialize in music — so we'd all have
some recreation in common. I think having a regular
music session once a day is even more important than
having Teague's gripe session, or meals together."

Peake stared at the floor. He said, "Look —" again,
and couldn't go on. Why was he here with all these
people he didn't really know and didn't want to know,
and the only person he had ever cared about, or ever
would care about, the other half of himself, at the other
end of a slowly lengthening separation which would
space out intolerably, in distance and time, until he
and Jimson were at opposite ends of a vast and lengthening nowhere. . . .

*Jimson's face, white and strained and tearful. You
don't care enough to stay,* he had flung at Peake, *I knew
we wouldn't both make Ship, but I thought you'd care
enough to stay. . . .*

But how could he have done that, after twelve years
of the finest education in the world, education that he,
a black kaffir from one of the kaffirland reserves in
South Africa, could never have had on his own con-
tinent. . . . UNEPS had given him this, and now it was
his turn to make some return to the only world he
knew. Fontana had voiced it; he wanted it out of his
power to have second thoughts. Only Jimson had not
been able to see it that way . . . there was no music he
could ever play again that would not have Jimson's face
tied into every note, gladness and sorrow and love and

sex and misery . . . he turned away toward the window opening on space and the returning space station, and said, "Let's talk about it some other time. All right?"

"No," Ching said, "that's the one thing we *can't* do — walk out on this kind of disagreement. Moira's right, we do need regular musical sessions, and we can't have them without you, Peake; that would take all the point out of having them. The whole purpose of making music together —"

Peake shrugged and dropped into a chair. The DeMag units were low enough in here that he did not sink into it, but he did not float away either. "Okay. No arguments."

"That's not the point —" Moira began.

"Hold it," Fontana said quietly, "I think this is turning into the first of those once-a-day sessions we agreed to have, and I think we need it out into the open. We start holding back on gripes and grievances, trying to be too polite, and we'll get explosions. Ching, you said something earlier that made me really angry; you said you'd hoped for Chris or Mei Mei or Fly or, as you put it, somebody with some computer sense; and here's Peake sulking because he doesn't have Jimson to play duets with —"

"*I am not sulking!*" Peake yelled, with such violence that he bobbed up from the surface of his chair in the light gravity.

"I know what Fontana's driving at," Moira said, "I think we ought to make it a rule that we don't talk about anyone — anyone we left behind. They're dead to us, whatever happens. Let the past go."

"I refuse to do that," Ravi said. "We need to remember. We need roots, a sense of our past. We have a right to remember."

"To remember, yes," Fontana said, "but not to hurt

each other making comparisons with people who aren't here — people we never had to meet under this kind of strain. People who might, or might not, have turned out more congenial than the ones we have. Look, all six of us are going to be together for a long, long time; close-quarters together, hothouse together, too damn much together; and the one thing we don't need is to rub elbows with the idealized memories of people who aren't here!"

"Now listen —" Peake began, but Moira went on:

"No, you listen, I'm not finished. I don't even mean you, personally. I'm trying to establish a principle, not get personal about anybody. I think every one of us could have picked what they'd consider a perfect crew, and somehow I doubt if any one of us would have picked any one of the others here —"

"What you mean is, you wouldn't," Ching said precisely. "Nice to know what you think of us, Moira."

She brushed that aside too. "I refuse to get into a fight with you, Ching, don't try to provoke it. I mean, here we are, six of us, none of us consulted about our preferences for the others —"

"They must have taken compatibility into account," Teague said. "I doubt if they would pick six people they knew couldn't stand one another!"

Moira shrugged. "Oh, I'm sure they trusted us not to murder each other, took real antipathies into account. But —"

Ching wasn't so sure. She said in a low voice, "I think they chose people who had demonstrated that they could conform if they had to."

"But whatever they decided," Moira said, "we are here. It's like those arranged marriages they used to have, hundreds of years ago, it's done and can't be undone. What God, or the Academy, has joined together, let no man put asunder. The six of us are here, and there are no others, and we'd better work out a way to care about each other; because there's nobody else for any of us, and we are not going to get any second chances!"

That, Peake thought, was laying it right out on the line, putting into words what they all knew and which he, at least, had never really faced. He set his jaw tight and said, "All right. Agreed."

"Agreed," Ching said promptly, adding, "I was out of line."

Peake said, "I'll play anything you want me to. But we'd better pick an hour which will work for the day people and the night people both, unless somehow our internal rhythms adjust. Which they might, at this distance — I don't think anyone really has tested circadian rhythms over long periods of time in zero-gee or alternating gravities. There might be some studies in the computer library, done on the Moon or space station. Meanwhile, I tend to be a day person myself, but I'm not extreme about it one way or the other."

But while the others were discussing the optimum time of an arbitrary day for the shared music session, Peake sat silent, watching the space station go and return in its orbit across their window — they were still in orbit around it.

It had been a flea-brained idea anyhow, the commitment he had made with Jimson. Dimly, he knew they had both been too young for the kind of lifetime commitment they had wanted to make. He had scorned people like Fly and Moira and Chris, whose wholesale sexual experimentation had been close to the promiscuous, but he knew he had gone to an equally dangerous other extreme; he had been so wrapped up in Jimson that he had made too few other friends.

*I'm not the only one. There's Ching, I don't think she
did any experimenting at all, she must be as lonely as
I am . . . or worse. But she's used to it . . . it was her
choice, and I. . . .* Then he recognized that as self-pity
and cut it off.

"You play the viola, don't you, Ching?"

"Violin, too," she said, nodding, "but I thought it
would be interesting to specialize in an instrument no
one else plays very often."

"There isn't much solo literature for it."

"True," Ching said, "but then, I'm not interested in
being a solo performer, and it got me a place in a lot
of string quartets. Because I'm a good violist, not a
second-rate violinist trying to play the viola."

Humility, Peake wondered, or a very shrewd assess-
ment of the kind of team-oriented thinking they'd want
on the Ship? Had Ching gambled, cleverly, for a place
in the most exclusive string quartet of all?

Fontana watched them talking agreeably about Mozart and Beethoven quartets, improvisational jazz sessions, and wondered if this was the final test, one called
survival; how they sorted themselves out, no guide-
lines, no rules. She might be the Ship's psychologist,
but Moira had forestalled the first suggestion she might
have made in that capacity — making it a firm rule that
the past should not be used as a defense against the
present. Peake might have agreed not to talk about Jimson; but could anyone stop him from brooding? Would
he be able to put it aside, would he need help, would
she be able to give it if he did?

And it was Peake who broke into a discussion of the
technique for synthesizing violin strings by saying,
"But now that we've settled the important things, like
the make-up of our string quartet, can we try discussing
a couple of very minor things, like where we are going,

and when do we leave? What's the procedure?''

"I think," Moira said, "we've had all the orders we're going to get. When we're ready to go, we just go, and that's that."

"Go *where*?" Ching asked. "Do we plot a course at random?"

"That's up to you," Ravi said, "you have the computer library. You know where planets have been found and colonized, you should make the decision about whether we try for a planet in an area where habitable planets have already been found, or whether we head in a new direction, where we'd have a chance at finding new, wholly untouched stars."

"I can only get that information on the Bridge," Ching said. "Has everyone had enough to eat?"

As they went back, one by one, through the dizzying shifts in gravity orientation — this time they were prepared for it and no one lost balance — Fontana reflected that already they had exercised the human habit of naming things; the room with consoles and computation equipment had become the Bridge, by analogy with a ship at sea, in spite of the fact that none of them had ever been on a naval ship. Still, she was glad that the vast observation window, with its lenticular view of half the visible universe, was opaqued against the endless stars; there was only a pale reflection of the colored winking lights on the control panels. Ching slid into a seat before the computer; Peake glanced at his chronometer and said to Ravi, "Toss you for day shift."

Ravi raised his eyebrows. "Why? You clearly prefer day shift; I unquestionably prefer night. Why risk committing each of us to our least favorite time? If we had the same preference, it would make some sense . . ."

Peake shrugged. "We'll run on Greenwich Time for

ship operations; Mean Solar Time for navigation. It's
1409 hours; day shift from 0800 to 2000 okay with
you?"

"Fine," said Ravi, and Peake slipped into the seat
before the navigation controls. Moira was already in
the drive seat. Fontana noticed there were ten seats
built into the control-room which they had called the
Bridge. She took one of them. Ravi sat where he could
see what Peake was doing. Teague was bending over
Moira, studying the control drives with interest.

Moira said, "The drives are ready to go; the only
question is, where. We have to leave the Solar System
in the direction we're intending to end up — I don't
have to tell you that. Where are we going, Ching?"

Ching stared at the printout on the greenish console
before her, navigation co-ordinates of the known colonies; and blindly up at the opaqued star-screen. The
whole universe lay before them — and they expected
her to make that decision? She said in a low voice,
"You're asking me to play God," and something in her
voice communicated her sense of awe, of immensity,
to Ravi. She had always been so aloof, so much in
command of herself, that Ravi, too, was shaken.

Did she feel it, too, that wonderment? he asked himself, and because Ching had always repelled any too-
personal approach, Ravi knew he could not ask.

He glanced at the opaqued star-glass, thinking of the
crowding immensity of the stars beyond. Unexplored
territory. A universe at their feet. Fragments; a scant
half dozen colonies out there, millions of billions of
stars, and the six of them in their frail little ship, to
find a habitable planet in all that wilderness. . . .

He said, and he heard his voice shaking, "I read somewhere, once, that for man to map and explore space
was as if a colony of mudfish in a waterhole in the

outback of Australia should map the coastline of Australia and every rock in the Greater Barrier Reef."

Only with the help of God, he thought; *mankind alone could never have done it.* And he knew that if he had said it aloud they would all have mocked him; so he was silent.

Teague looked at Ravi, sympathetically. He had gone through this during his first year in the study of astronomy. Facing the indifference of enormous galaxies, the smallness of his own kind against the universe. He said, good-naturedly, "Well, this colony of mudfish has done it. And Ching has the results in the computer. Which way, Ching?"

They were all looking at her now. She said, trying to make her voice matter-of-fact, "I don't think it's fair to ask me to make a decision of that size. Not when it affects all of you. I honestly think this is the place for Moira's consensus decision."

"You're the one with the information," Teague said, "and you were the one who seemed, a while ago, to be in favor of command decisions. What does it matter which way we go? As long as we stay out of black holes, we're just as likely — speaking from statistic analysis — to find a habitable planet in one direction as in the next."

Moira exploded. "How can you say that, Teague? Are you saying we can stick a pin in a star-map — or whatever the equivalent would be in the computer — and pick a direction at random?"

"Not at all," Teague said, "I'm simply pointing out that whatever way we go, we are equally likely, or unlikely, to find a good planet, or not to find one."

Peake said, "It would seem sensible to go in the direction where we know colonies have already been established, observe the conditions near there, and go on to found neighbor colonies by mapping and surveying the next dozen star-systems or so."

"That at least gives us a place to start," Fontana said, "and it would make for an orderly approach."

"And I'm willing to bet," Moira said, "that the last fifty or sixty Ships have done exactly that."

"Why shouldn't they?" Ching asked. "It seems the logical thing to do."

"We'll never know," Teague said, "because we are Survey Ship one hundred and three. The colonies were founded, as I remember, by year-ships seven, ten, eleven, and nineteen. The crews of those Ships are probably in their thirties or forties by now — I'd have to figure out the time-dilatation equations, and I don't have them on the tip of my tongue the way Ravi probably does — but we have no news of any later Ships, though ships twenty-four and twenty-five could, theoretically, be reporting any day now. Depending on where they went; and we may or may not ever know that."

"Which is one reason for heading toward an established colony," said Peake. "It might be our only chance for any contact with the human race again in our lifetime."

"You're talking as if we were going to age at Earth-time," Teague said. "As we approach light-speed, our age will slow down and for us, biologically speaking, time will virtually stop. Of course we can't be sure we'll see them for years, unless we choose to visit one of the established colonies first. But I think we're expected to find a planet and report it ready for colonization first. Then we can visit already-established colonies, and by that time there will certainly be others."

Peake thought; even *if I could ever come back, Jimson*

would be an old man and I still young. He had known
that, intellectually. Now it became suddenly personal,
and frightening. And meaningful, with a horrible personal meaning that left him speechless, staring into the
console of the navigation instruments.

"I still think it makes sense to explore outward from
the known colonies, in an orderly fashion," Ravi said.
"We should stay in contact with the known human
settlements; otherwise the chances we'd ever run across
one by accident — well, the old needle in a haystack
analogy would be very good odds by comparison."

"But if we find a planet in a wholly new direction,"
Moira argued, "then humanity can spread in that many
more new directions without being wholly lost. We'd
establish a new beachhead in the Galaxy —"

"You're speaking as if this were a military conquest,"
Fontana said.

"Well, it is, in a sense," Moira said, "us against an
empty universe, and we're going and making new paths
for ourselves —"

"As we did in America and Australia?" Ravi asked
dryly, "by wiping out the Amerinds and the aborig-
ines?"

"We haven't found any trace of intelligent life anywhere," Moira said. "There was none anywhere in the
Alpha Centaurus system, and none on any of Wolf 459's
five planets. We may just be alone in the entire Galaxy."

"I find that approach thoroughly offensive," Fontana
said, "that we have the right to do whatever we please,
anywhere, just because we have the technology to come
and take over —"

Teague said, ironically, "I thought one of the reasons
for getting out into space was to be free of you ecological
nuts who want the planet left in perfectly unspoiled
primitive conditions!"

"Look, none of this is relevant," Ching said sharply. "We can debate our various philosophical positions at our leisure, for the next four light-years or so at least! Just now we have to decide in which direction we leave the Solar System!"

"And we asked you to decide that," Peake said.

"And I told you then, and I tell you again, I will not play God that way! For a decision this big, we need a consensus!"

"You were telling us, a while ago, that we should choose a commander and let the commander make those decisions," Fontana argued, "and then when we ask you to take that responsibility, you cop out and demand a group consensus!"

Ching felt overwhelmed by the hostility in Fontana's voice. Somehow she had felt that if she won a place on the final crew she would have proved her right to belong, she would have been accepted. Now she realized that nothing had changed; she was simply alone within the smaller group of hostile strangers, that was all. But still alone.

She said quietly, "I don't think you understood me, Fontana. Certainly, if you all agree that it is my decision to make, I'll make it, but I don't think, at this moment, that I have enough information. Moira, you want to establish a new beachhead for mankind — no, wait, we'll argue over definitions later — and Ravi, I think, suggested heading for the known colonies and exploring outward from there in an orderly fashion."

"I agree with Ravi," Peake said, "somehow I doubt if our Survey Ships have managed to find every habitable planet in that quarter of the Galaxy."

Fontana said, "There's good reason for going in that direction. Before the first Survey Ship left, a hundred and five years ago, they surveyed everything they could from Base One on Alpha Centaurus, and decided it was the most promising area to find new planets and probably intelligent life — or conditions favoring it."

Teague said, diffidently, "Considering that we have a good deal of information about that part of the Galaxy, isn't it time some crew explored in another direction, and started feeding back information?"

"I don't think that's the point of the Survey Ships," Peake argued. "We were sent to find a habitable planet, not to add to the general sum total of information. The best place to look for new planets is where planets have already been found."

Moira demanded, "Why should we do just what other ships have done?"

Ching raised her smooth eyebrows. "Why not?"

"We have here," said Ravi, "the ultimate difference between the pure scientist and the applied scientist; to find new information about the nature of the universe, or to apply that information to use by mankind. Personally, I think the Academy is applied science; we were given orders to find a planet, not find out new things about the universe. Our job is to find a new planet, and I think we owe it to them. After all —" suddenly his voice cracked, "we'll certainly find out new things, wherever we go. There's — there's plenty to find, out — out there."

Fontana thought, with detachment, *he's scared. After twelve years of supervision in the Academy, we're all scared to death of being on our own. But we've got to get used to it.*

Moira, with that eerie responsiveness, almost telepathic, asked, "Isn't all this delay just a way of trying to cling to some — some lifeline of the familiar? Are we afraid to take off into the unknown?"

"If we are," said Ching, "I don't think it will do us

any good, not in the long run. For what it's worth, I agree with Peake and Ravi; the best place to look for a shell is on the beach, and the best place to look for a planet is where it's been demonstrated that there are many of them."

Teague said, "Creation doesn't differ from one quarter of the universe to another. It all came from the Big Bang and if there are planets in one place, there are certain to be planets in any other."

Ching asked, "Do we have a clear majority, then? Peake, Ravi, Fontana, and I prefer to proceed toward previously established colonies; Moira and Teague vote for a new and unknown direction —"

Teague shook his head. "I was commenting about the nature of the universe, not voting. I'm willing to go along with the majority."

"As far as that goes, so am I," Moira said. "My objection was purely philosophical; I don't approve of majority decisions or majority rule. Historically speaking, democracy is the worst tyranny ever invented by humanity — if we'd left it to majority rule, Peake's people would still be slaves, we'd all have been brought up praying in school, and there would never have been a space program at all. Majorities always settle for the lowest common denominator and the rule of the uninformed."

Ching's eyebrows went up again. She said, "Are you going to take the part of the philosophical rebel among us, Moira, always taking the minority position just to prevent any consensus decision?"

Moira's freckled face flushed bright pink. She said, "I don't think that's a fair way of putting it, Ching."

"No? How would you put it, then?"

Fontana, watching in silence, realized that this was the first head-to-head confrontation any of them had known. The discipline of the Academy, the knowledge that open hostility would not be tolerated, had down-played this kind of thing since they were kindergarten age. Should she intervene, tactfully, to defuse it; was this her job as the only psychologist on the crew?

Damn it, she thought, *no! Not me!* And faced the knowledge that, although she had been crammed with knowledge of psychology, she was only seventeen years old, and no more a psychologist than Peake, with all his knowledge of surgery, was a surgeon. At seventeen they had the rudimentary knowledge of their profes-sions, but they didn't have the experience or knowledge which, alone, could qualify them for their chosen professions.

And there's no way to yell for help when we find we can't handle it! God, the Academy is ruthless! They know that only young people can survive long enough to do their work at interstellar distances, so they throw us out to sink or swim! Is that why so many crews go out and are never heard of again?

Ching still looked angry. She said, "Obviously I'm not going to give any command to take the ship any-where over your dead body, Moira. What I need to know is whether your objection means, 'I am unalter-ably opposed to going in the direction other ships have gone,' or whether it means, 'I am opposed to majority rule for philosophical reasons but in this particular case I am willing to work with the majority.' I would like to say that, speaking from that philosophical po-sition you were talking about, I don't find majority rule very satisfactory either. Which is why I felt one person ought to have command authority to make last-ditch decisions if a consensus *can't* be found."

Moira's flush slowly subsided. She said, "In that case, Ching, I withdraw my objections. I admit I'd like to take off in a direction humanity has never gone before. On the other hand, I don't think they gave us this ship to satisfy our intellectual curiosity about the universe, either. I'll agree with the others; we go in the direction of known colonies."

Ching said, "In that case I'll get information about navigation co-ordinates for the known colonies, and we'll head for the most recent of them . . . right, Peake?"

Fontana felt they were all relieved to have avoided a real confrontation. This meant, at the constant rate of acceleration, they would not have to make any more major policy decisions for more than a year, perhaps four or five years just under the speed of light.

And if we can't figure out a way to make them by then, we'll deserve everything that happens to us.

Teague grinned shyly. He said, "I don't have the exact co-ordinates in my head, but it means, I know, that we'll be heading out past Saturn's place in orbit. And we'll get a good close look at it — which I always wanted. Granted the telemetered shots are pretty spectacular; but I always wanted to see it from within a million miles or so."

Ching said absently, her fingers working on the computer console, "If we head for Colony Five, that will bring us out within two hundred thousand miles of Saturn's rings. We could make it a little closer, but that would mean altering course to avoid coming within orbital distance of one of the moons —"

"Japetus," Ravi said absently, looking over Ching's shoulder.

Teague demanded, "How the hell do you *do* that, Ravi?"

His dark face flushed. "I'm not sure," he said, "I never did know *how* I do it. It just adds up in my head."

Ching said formally, "The co-ordinates are on the

console. You can work out a course, Peake, and
then, I suppose, it's Moira's business to cut the drives
in — "

Peake looked around, hesitantly. "So that's all there
is to it? We simply — go? Just like that? Shouldn't
we — let them know, or something? As a courtesy?"

"Courtesy from whom to whom?" Moira asked. "Face
it; they don't expect to hear from us again until we
bring them a habitable planet. They've kicked the baby
birds right out of the nest."

It's all gone, Peake thought. *All the life any of us
have ever had, until this moment. And Jimson.* He
touched the button which cleared the huge window,
letting the stars blaze into the control cabin.

"Don't," Moira said, turning her eyes away, "it makes
me dizzy. I think we have to — to get used to it. In
stages."

"We'd better get used to it," Peake said, savagely,
"because it's all there is. All we've got. Any of us. Just
what's out there. And we might as well learn to face
it now as later! There's no sense staying in the womb!"

CHAPTER FOUR

Ching felt, still, that there ought to be more to it than this — some formal report to the Space Station that Survey Ship #103 was on its way, some acknowledgement, some formal leave-taking. But they had had all that when they were chosen as a crew ... it was foolish to wish for more. She kept her eyes down on the steady familiar console of the Bridge computer, the numbers and letters which appeared as she touched buttons. She had done this on a similar console many times during her training, and since they had decided to take their course toward the most recent of the colonies, even the course was one she had plotted before. It seemed almost too simple.

Since there was no other formality possible, she made her voice formal.

"Colonies one and two are in the system of Barnard's Star, at six light-years distance. Colony Three is at Cygni 61; eleven light-years distance. Colony Four is in the Sirius double-star system, eight point eight light-years, and Colony Six is established in the T-5 cluster, nine point three light-years distance."

"And," said Teague, "it's very probable that when we get to the T-5 cluster, if that's where we are going, we will find Colonies Seven through Eleven — maybe through twenty or twenty-four — established there, with no planets left for us."

Peake shrugged. "Then we start hunting from there, I suppose."

Moira said, "If we leave the Solar System in that direction, that means we'll be off the plane of the ecliptic and we'll miss the asteroids. No way we're maneuverable enough to get through the asteroid belt without being crashed by a minor asteroid. We could program the ship to avoid the bigger, better-known ones, the more predictable ones, but there are hundreds of thousands of them — maybe millions."

"I have the precise number of known bodies in the computer," Ching said, "but does anyone really care?"

"I do," said Teague, "but it's irrelevant right now."

Peake looked at the readout from Ching's computer on the panel before him. He frowned, flicking buttons on the pocket calculator at his belt, then started to lay in a course in the general direction of the T-5 cluster. It was still day-shift; Ravi sat behind him, with nothing, at the moment, to do except watch Peake's huge, clumsy-looking hands on the buttons and switches. The fingers were so long, and so large, that they obscured the switches at times.

It was almost frightening to contemplate this kind of freedom, this kind of distance. He did not mind the vista of stars outside the transparent glass dome . . . although he noticed that Moira kept her eyes carefully turned away from it.

Navigating on the surface of the Earth, there were three-hundred-and-sixty directions in which you could go, and some of that was limited by features of the terrain — mountains, water, heavy undergrowth, pre-existing roads. In the air you had the full three hundred sixty degrees; he'd grown used to that, flying a light plane.

But out here there were all those directions, multiplied into three dimensions . . . 360 to the three-sixtieth power, maybe? Up, down, and all the permutations and combinations of angles in between.

The universe is too big . . . thank God we have the computer . . . all the crowding multiplicity of stars, vastness beyond imagining . . . we talk glibly of light-years. But the light from the Sun takes eight minutes to reach Earth. Think of something so distant that the light takes a year, a whole year, to reach it . . . that's a light-year . . . the simple explanation he had been given in kindergarten, their whole education aimed at making these monstrous things close and simple and familiar and comfortable. . . .

Ravi shut his eyes, to shut out the thousand blinking lights of the bridge, and the millions of blinking stars behind it. There was just too much of it. These distances were not made by man at all, man could not envision them. The mudfish in the water hole in the outback had mapped the Great Barrier Reef . . . but was this arrogance, was it meant that mankind should do this?

Behind his closed eyes pictures formed, faces in a crowded Bombay slum, starving faces, packed filthy faces; but he had grown up clean and well-fed, educated almost beyond human possibility, to do a deed at the very limits of the possible. *Why me, why was I chosen with these others? Why millions to starve and die and bumble along from day to‘day, and the six of us to live in luxury and attain the limits of human possibility? Dare I think that the Great Architect of the Universe has chosen me? Is it any better to think that it was the work of random Chaos and chance?*

He knew he could go mad this way, and opened his eyes, fastening them on the navigation console. His eyes slid past Peake to Moira, and, trying to wrench his mind away from vastnesses too great to contemplate, he forced himself to think of the mundane and familiar. Moira. He had, briefly, been one of her lovers. Somehow he had begun to think, seeing Peake and Jimson, separated, that they had chosen a crew with no sexual ties to one another. He thought, trying to control an unseemly laugh, that it would have been hard to find any man in her year who had not been, at least briefly, Moira's lover. No, he didn't think was promiscuous, though one or two of the women were, but she had experimented widely, and she was a friendly girl with no special sexual inhibitions; he thought that Teague, for instance, had also been chosen, a year or so ago, to share Moira's favors.

Was she thinking about that? he wondered. Two ex-lovers on the Ship? It was simpler to lose himself into a frankly erotic reverie than to contemplate that painful vastness outside the ship, or to try and wrestle some meaning for it all from the unyielding cosmos.

Moira was not thinking about anyone, or anything, human, at all. The faint apprehension she felt, she forced down into calm; she told herself that the view from outside the dome made her dizzy, with all the stars, the Space Station moving sedately past their window every few seconds, disturbing her visual orientation. When she closed her eyes she felt quite comfortable, her stomach in place, the DeMag gravitation strong enough so that she did not lose her up-down orientation with the control board.

Peake said, "Well, it's like one of those old Navy novels — should I yell out 'Engineer, set all sails' . . . "

"You're mixing your metaphors," Fontana said. "In the days when they set sails, in the Navy, they didn't have engineers." She too was in one of the supernu-

merary seats; they had all chosen to be present for that
moment when Survey Ship 103 moved away from the
Space Station. From being as nearly at rest as any body
in the universe could be — moving in free-fall orbit
around the Space Station — they would begin their
long, slow, but steady acceleration which, within a
year, would bring them to 99.3 per cent of light-speed;
the highest practical speed for space travel. And so
rapid would this acceleration be that, from just outside
the orbit of the Moon, they would leave Pluto's orbit
behind within thirteen days.

Moira wet her lips, checked the panel before her,
then, deliberately, touching the buttons with gentle fingers, she pressed a certain sequence which would ac-
tivate the drives. Although the drive was in another
module, and the intervening total vacuum of space
would not convey even a fragment of sound, she fancied that she could feel a faint vibration, somewhere,
the drives setting up their vibration . . . not a sound.
Not a vibration. Had it to do with her extra-sensory
perception, so that she felt it somewhere inside herself,
that the drives were running, like a heartbeat?

She checked the green light on the console which
telemetered information, looked at a small visual panel
which gave video information from the drive module.
There were, of course, no moving parts, but energy was
being transmitted, and outside the dome window, the
Space Station began to recede, grow smaller against the
background of stars. It was no longer passing their window every few seconds. It was moving away . . . no.
They were moving away, Survey Ship 103 was accelerating away from the Space Station at nine point eight
meters per second per second. . . . at an ever-increasing
velocity. Moira was not the natural mathematician Ravi
was, and could not keep track of the continuing veloc-

ity without flicking a glance at the tell-tales giving velocity, and the percentage of *Tau* — light-speed.

"There it goes," Fontana said suddenly. "We might
as well take a last look."

Earth had come into their viewfield, a dim blue
wraith, the size of a small dinnerplate, diminishing,
distant . . . a raindrop. Moira blinked, shook the tears
from her eyes, concentrating on the drive tell-tale. Now,
when they were clear of the last fragments of gravita-
tional pull from the Moon and from the Space Station . . now, slowly, gently . . . she pressed another
sequence of buttons in a memorized order, feeling the
faint drag from the DeMag units; possibly it would be
easier when they could turn off the DeMags for a while,
but at this moment none of them were emotionally or
physiologically prepared for less than half gravity. The
ship rotated, modules turning for favorable light ex-
posure. She watched what she was doing on her video
tell-tales as the light-sail panels, enormous, thin sheets
of mylar film, were slowly extruded. She could see a
corner of one of them coming, slowly, into sight across
the dome, a smear of translucence blotting out a few
of the stars across the lower edge of the lenticular observation window. *Trim it just a little toward the sun,*
Moira thought, pressing buttons gently, watching the
sail veer ever so slightly, rotate a little, streaming
gently. Her tell-tales told her of other sails, great sheets
of film sensitive to solar pressure . . . light as a tangible
force, making the sails just shiver . . . the film was so
delicate it would tear at a touch, but in space, friction-
less, airless, there was nothing to tear it. Yet Moira's
fingers moved as delicately on the studs as if her fingers
could rip through the sails themselves, and she watched
the movement, the imperceptible shiver of the streaming mylar, with a lump in her throat. *That's right, just*

*a fraction more to the left . . . now you, back there by
the Life-Support module . . . come on, darling, easy
now . . . just a little further . . .* she was whispering to
the sails as they moved, slowly and with a silken el-
egance, into position. She felt like a spider, spinning
out her silken web into every direction, surrounded by
the feathery streaming of filmy sails, responding to the
light . . . feeding the endless energies of light into the
drives. The awareness shimmered inside her nerves
with the violence of orgasm, and she closed her eyes
in momentary ecstasy.

Teague watched Moira's face quivering as she moved
her hands on the controls, and remembered how she
had looked, once, when he kissed her . . . he himself
felt as useless as a vermiform appendix. Life-Support
was fail-safe and idiot-proof; barring some unimagin-
able catastrophe, he would have nothing important to
do for years, except for synthesizing food. When, or if,
they found a habitable planet — when, not if, he reminded himself sternly — it would be quite different;
as the biologist, he would be responsible for every fragment of their physical safety in an alien environment.
Aboard ship, he had a sinecure; he was a piece of dis-
pensable software, whose work was being done by
machinery and computer.

Well, they were all like that, really. The ship could
have been sent out, unmanned, as a probe — but an
unmanned probe could not have surveyed the planets
at the hypothetical other end of the voyage. Only Peake,
as their doctor, and Fontana, as their psychologist,
would have much to do on the voyage of nine light-
years. Once they were out of the Solar System, only
Moira would have much of anything to do inside the
ship, and that was mostly trimming the sails by cal-

culating light-pressures. The ship would navigate on a course which Peake and Ching had already set; to change it now would mean decelerating down to zero and re-computing from the beginning. Every second they remained in flight, they were reaching velocities which were more and more unthinkable. More than nine meters per second per second — maybe Ravi could have figured out how fast they were actually travelling by now. He couldn't.

So the most interesting thing he'd be doing for the next several years was synthesizing catgut for violin strings!

Perhaps he would have time to learn to play the oboe — there were spare instruments aboard. Or he would have time to compose the string quartet which had been in his mind ever since he learned, at fourteen, that he did not have the manual dexterity to be more than a mediocre violinist, and taken up the flute. Melodies moved constantly in his mind; now he would have time to write them down.

He'd never tried before; most music was computer-written. He remembered a story from the early days of the Academy, when the computer, programmed to write a chorale, had exactly duplicated, missing only four notes in the tenor part, Bach's setting for *O Sacred Head*. Well, given the information about how to compose music, that *was* the perfect chorale, the logical and perfect way to write and harmonize the music, the inevitability of perfection. The people who programmed the computer had been overwhelmed by Bach, after all; and after that episode the Melody Mark VII had been nicknamed JOHANN.

How could anyone write music greater than that, or worth naming in the same breath? Well, the twentieth-century classic composer Alan Hovhaness had done it;

critics had said that he had taken music in the direction
it might have gone if Bach had never written his *Well-
Tempered Clavier*. Perhaps there were still other directions, though he was sure Peake didn't think so, and
Peake was a real musician.

Now the Earth could barely be distinguished; it had
lost its blue color and was a point of light against black,
against other points of light. Ravi glanced at his chronometer and said, "My shift, Peake." Peake drew his
attention from the window and said, "Right." Formally,
they exchanged places. Teague said, "Are we going to
keep on Greenwich Time for the whole voyage? Hours,
days . . . weeks, months, years — they don't make much
sense out here. Anyhow, as we approach light-speed,
there'll be changes . . . it's not as if we could keep the
clock set for what time it is back in dear old Greenwich
of whatever!"

Peake said, turning his back on the vista of stars —
that was Ravi's responsibility for the next twelve
hours — "We have to keep a 24 hour ship's day, or
something near it. For circadian rhythms. God alone
knows what light-speeds and zero gravity will do to
our body rhythms. But we have to try and keep them
as stable as we can, and for the next few months it
won't matter much."

"The ship's already on Universal Solar," Ravi said,
looking at a small tell-tale at the very center of the
ceiling of the Bridge; the seats swivelled through a full
circular rotation — so they could be turned to any angle, though they would lock at whatever angle the sitter
chose. The tell-tale displayed, in smooth-flowing liquid
crystal digital numbers the time by what was called
Universal Solar, or sometimes only *true time*; a kind
of reckoning in seconds from the pulses of energy,
elapsed time from the original Big Bang; true time, so-

called, measured the exact age of the known Universe.

"But Universal Solar is clumsy," said Peake, looking at the long stream of numbers which measured time, in seconds, from the beginning of the universe.

"Clumsy!" Moira said, disbelieving, and Ching said, "How can anything as precise as that be clumsy?"

"Because," Peake said, good-naturedly, "by the time you read all that off, in seconds, it's some other time already. I suggest we keep Greenwich Time just to figure out when our shifts begin and end, and when we're going to meet for those daily music sessions Fontana, or was it Moira, thought were so important."

Looking at the long, ever-changing stream of numbers on the tell-tale, they all, one by one, agreed to that. Greenwich Time would become a kind of biological time-clock for them; Ching's flying fingers programmed, into the computer, a sequence of "elapsed time, in hours and days, from leaving the space station," basing it on 24-hour days, of which this — they all agreed — was Day One. Years calculated in Earth reckoning, *Anno Domini*, a religio-political reckoning, they all agreed, had no meaning for them. Day One became the day they had been skylifted, first to the Space Station, then to the Ship; and by that reckoning, when Ravi took his first shift, it became noon of Day One. Peake would go on-shift again at Midnight, which they would call the first moment of Day Two.

"And we have been aboard for four hours," Ching said, "and my biological rhythms are beginning to tell me that it's dinner-time. Is there any reason we have to stay in the Bridge, or must one of us be here to tend the machines at all times? And what will that do to our theory that we all ought to meet once a day?"

Moira made a final finicky adjustment to a sail, a great triangular translucency blotting out a third of the

stars. From the lenticular window she could see that
the ship was rotating on its own axis as it moved against
the stars. They seemed to be standing still, now, without the reference points of Space Station and Earth,
and when she shut her eyes, the DeMag units told her
that "down" was the floor of the Bridge, and the lenticular window was straight before her; but when she
looked out to the small slow spin of the ship around
them, the other shaped modules that came into view
and were obscured again, themselves obscuring nearby
stars, she felt a trace of vertigo, her inner ear channels
rebelled, and she wondered how she could manage to
swallow against this queasiness. She shut her eyes and
the Bridge settled into homey normal up-and-down.
Stability again.

"Nobody has to be here," she said, looking with
tender farewell at the exquisite delicacy of the sail shivering across the stars, "the sails are programmed to trim
themselves; strictly speaking, we could leave the Bridge
now and spend the next four years or so playing string
quartets and making love in our cabins. Each of us
ought to check in here on our instruments once every
shift or so, but mostly that's busy-work. Once our
course is set, that's it." And she wondered why a faint,
sick shiver went through her at the words; and she
remembered her younger self, crying and refusing to
step on a piece of playground equipment which, a few
minutes later, cast several of her playmates, and one
of her counselors, to the ground in screaming heaps. . . .

Angrily, she dismissed the thought. *I'm tired and
sick and I think I have a touch of gravity sickness and
I'm making up nightmares and calling it ESP!* Because
there had been times when her erratic wild talent had
played her false, giving her a warning of trouble which
never happened, especially when there was something

she particularly wanted not to do.

Ching, accustomed from early childhood to rely on computer-set certainties, nodded at Moira's words. She said, "Actually, we're just along for the ride. The computers run the ship."

"Actually, I was thinking that myself," Teague said. "It seems that you and Moira are doing all the real work of the ship, and it might make more sense to put the four of us others into suspended animation. When we reached a planet, you could wake us up, we'd still be young and stronger than we would otherwise, and we could do the survey work on that planet . . . "

"I don't know about you," Moira said, "but I don't think I'd care to make a voyage of nine point something years to the T-5 cluster without more company than Ching. No offense intended, Ching, but it's a known psychological fact — Fontana, I'm right, aren't I? — that any two people alone together will drive each other crazy and murder each other."

Fontana chuckled. She said, "It has been known to happen. It's true; that's why the minimal crew for a Survey Ship has to be at least four people, and six is better. That gives everybody some privacy, and somebody new to talk to now and then. Even as it is, we're likely to get bored with each other's company."

Although Ching knew that Moira's words were not personally intended, she still felt somehow wounded. *But at least,* she thought, *they know that I — and the computer — have set the major work of the Ship. Peake plotted the co-ordinates and the course, but it was the computer which gave it to him. The computer and I.* Very precisely, intending to wound a little, she said, "I don't know about you, Moira, I can well understand that you might need a certain amount of diversion on a long voyage, but I think it would be interesting to experiment with a Survey Ship staffed by one human and one computer. I would gladly have volunteered for such a voyage. I'm not afraid of my own company, and I don't need to hide from it. With this computer — " and only Moira saw, and understood, the affectionate touch of her fingers on the console, " — I don't really think I would need anyone else on the voyage. After all, I went through the Academy as a loner, and I'm used to it."

Ravi looked at the immensity beyond the window and said, "We are all alone, fundamentally, with the universe — " but he said it so softly that no one else heard.

Moira stood up and went to Ching. She said, very gently, "But you weren't alone, and I think if you were *really* alone, with the computer, you'd go crazy. I know *I* would."

"I know you would, too," Ching said, stiff against the friendly arm Moira slid around her waist, and Moira sighed and let her go. It was, after all, impossible to be friendly with Ching. She had tried it before, and been rebuffed in the same way, and here she was, stuck with her for the indefinite future.

Ching, her face tightly barriered, was thinking, *Oh, yes, Moira, being nice to the class freak, the way she'd be so nice to a cripple or a blind person. Well, I'm damned if I want her pitying me!* She said, "Well, the question's academic anyhow. It makes more sense to figure out who's going to cook dinner. Teague, didn't you say there was fresh food storage for a period of months? Why don't we celebrate our takeoff with a steak dinner, or the nearest equivalent we can find in the food machines? I'll volunteer to cook tonight, but after this we take turns."

Once again, the dizzying shifts in direction as they
moved from the strongly oriented gravity of the "bridge"
to the Life-Support central area — which was fairly
circular — and once again Peake stumbled as the direction of "down" abruptly reversed itself.

Moira, flipping herself over in the low gravity, catch-
ing Ravi and spinning with him on a common center
in the almost-gravity-free corridor between two modules, thought, *I guess the gravity-sickness was psychological. When I don't have to look out that damned
window at the whole universe, I seem to have my
space-orientation just fine!* Holding tight to Ravi's
hand, they cartwheeled the length of the zero-gravity
corridor. Ching was clinging tightly to the crawl-bar,
inching like a fly along the wall. Peake pushed his legs
against one end and took off, shooting along the corridor and colliding with Ravi and Moira; the three of
them ended in a laughing tangle of arms and legs.
Teague and Fontana, clinging to each other and making
"swimming" motions, joined in the laughter.

"I should remind you all," Peake said, "that the exercise area — that's the conical module we didn't get
to, next to the sleeping quarters — is arranged with
DeMag units that can be cut down to zero or up to full
gravity. We have to work out at full gravity to keep our
muscles in good shape — " Teague groaned, but Peake
ignored him and went on, "but we can experiment with
free-fall acrobatics if we want to, too."

"Look at Ching," Moira squeaked. "Let go, Ching,
you can't get hurt, there's nowhere to fall to!"

Ching was clinging dizzily to the crawl-bar still. She
said, "I think I'll wait to get my orientation. If it's quite
all right with you, Moira?" she added meticulously.

Fontana's voice was sharp. "Let her alone, Moira, we all have to adjust at our own rate, and you've been in free-fall before; she hasn't."

Moira, holding to Ravi, felt his body against hers, looked with pleasure at the contrast of his coffee-colored hands against her own pallid ones. She twisted a little and their lips met; she felt his kiss with a shock of recognition, a familiar thing among all the new strangenesses. They floated together, their lips just touching, entangled, her hair floating around him, streaming, intermingled with his own dark curls. She fancied Ching's look down at them both was one of disapproval, and defiantly prolonged the kiss.

Peake pushed through the sphincter into the next module, which was the main cabin they had first entered. He went to the food machine, Ching joining him there a moment later.

Ching said, "They didn't lose any time, did they — Moira and Ravi?"

Peake shrugged. He said, "Does it matter that much?" The sight of the two, intertwined and kissing, lost in each other, roused painful memories. Every scrap of his being longed for Jimson; even during the excitement of pulling away from the Space Station, he had had to keep remembering, *I can't share it with him, is he watching me go, I'll never be able to share it with him again.* Was Jimson suffering like this, too, at the other end of that lengthening string which separated them? Part of him wanted Jimson to share even this suffering, part of him quailed at the thought of Jimson, tender, sweet, vulnerable, undergoing this monstrous pain that seemed to eat him up inside.

Alone, and I will be alone all the rest of my life. There is no one here for me. Both Ravi and Teague are obviously heterosexual, and as for the women I

*don't want them, they don't want me . . . alone. Always
alone, a lifetime alone. . . .*

Ching, standing beside him at the console, thought
that he looked lost; it was so strange to see Peake without the fair-haired Jimson trailing him.

*I know what it is to be alone. I went through twelve
years of it. But he at least has known what it is like to
be loved and wanted,* she thought disconsolately. *I
never will.*

She said, "Do you suppose we could manage a steak
dinner out of the console, Peake?"

"Can't hurt to try," he said, "it may not actually be
steak, but it will probably be too good an imitation for
me to tell the difference."

"We might have a little more trouble with the fried
potatoes and onion rings," she said, smiling. "And I
suspect fresh salads are always going to be beyond our
reach. Oh, well, Vitamin C is Vitamin C, I suppose."

Watching her hands move on the consoles, as surely
as they had moved upon the computer, Peake envied
her self-sufficiency.

*She doesn't need anybody. She has never had this
sense of being only half a person, only half alive, the
rest of the self moving away at nine point eight meters
per second per second . . .* it overwhelmed him to think
how far apart he was already from Jimson, separated
already by time as well as distance.

Ching slid open a panel; a savory smell emerged from
the inside. She said, "I hope you like your steak well
done."

"As a matter of fact," he said, chagrined, "I like it
rare, but I'll eat it any way it comes, Ching."

"I like it well done," Teague said, somersaulting
down from the spincter lock. "Ouch! Someday I'll have
to get used to where the gravity is in the different mod-

ules! Can I have that one, Ching, and you fix a rare one
for Peake? Don't tell me your friend the computer
mixed up the orders? I thought computers were infal-
lible!"

Ching shook her head, handing him the plate of well-
charred "steak."

"A computer," she said, glad to have something else
to think about, "is an idiot savant. It does just exactly
what it is told, and absolutely nothing it is not told to
do. It's only as intelligent as the person who programs
it — and the person who uses it. It could have all the
knowledge of the universe inside — " she waved at the
console of the food processor, "and it wouldn't be a bit
of good unless somebody knew exactly the right instructions to give it, put into the computer in exactly
the right way. I must have put in the wrong input —
I thought I had it marked for rare, because I tend to
digest proteins better when they're somewhat under-
coagulated — but it came out well done. But the computer isn't at fault, only the instructions I gave it. A
computer is *exactly* like an idiot savant. Remember the
little boy they had on one of the training films we saw?
He was blind, autistic, and couldn't be toilet-trained,
but at the age of nine he could add a column of ninety
figures in his head. He didn't know how he did it —
in fact, he couldn't be *asked* how he did it, because he
seemed to understand numbers, but not verbal speech
concepts. But you put in numbers and he would come
up with the right answer." As Ravi came in, still in-
terlaced with Moira, handing her carefully down into
the change of gravity in the DeMag units, she asked,
"Is that how you do your lightning-calculation, Ravi?
I can understand an autistic idiot doing that — he has
nothing *else* to occupy his mind — but you're highly
intelligent and verbal too. Yet you compute automati-

cally, in the same way as that autistic idiot-savant."

"I wish I knew, Ching," Ravi said. "All I can say is that old *cliché* from psychology — a normal person uses five per cent of his brain cells, the greatest geniuses maybe five per cent more than that. The other ninety per cent — well, who knows what's inside it? Wild talents like Moira's ESP, or mine, or the idiot-savant's. Maybe anything, maybe nothing. Who knows? Who cares? Thank you, Ching," he added, taking a plate with a sizzling chunk of rare meat on it, "this is perfect."

"I'll have one just like it for you in five seconds, Peake," Ching promised. "Is yours done well enough, Teague? How would you like yours cooked, Fontana?" She felt a surge of pleasure; they might not like her, but at this moment she was catering to their enjoyment, she was useful to them.

Ravi and Moira, still entwined loosely, ate, feeding each other choice bites from their plates. Teague and Fontana chatted, smiling.

"You're a harpsichordist, a pianist, Fontana. And of course the weight problem, lifting a piano or harpsichord from Earth, would be impossible. But you have an electronic keyboard, don't you?"

She nodded. "They warned me about that when I decided to specialize in keyboard music," she said, "that any career off-planet would mean abandoning almost everything I'd done in music."

"It should be possible to *build* a harpsichord," Teague mused. "We've certainly got *time* enough, and we can machine any parts we want to very precise tolerances. Building here on shipboard, we can synthesize the materials . . . "

She shrugged. "I can play recorder and flute some, and an electronic keyboard will do for accompaniment," she said, "and I never had any serious ambitions as a solo instrumentalist. It isn't as if I'd had a talent like Zora's. *That* kind of talent sweeps away everything else. Nobody with that much musical talent would have cared whether they made Ship or not, and of course they wouldn't —"

"I don't think it's a question of *talent*," Moira said, "Mei Mei had a voice as good as Zora's. What she didn't have was the drive, the ambition if you like. It isn't talent that makes a performer. It's desire — what a person wants more than anything in the world. I think all six of us wanted to make the Ship more than anything else, and we had more drive and ambition than the ones who turned up second to us."

"I'm not so sure," Fontana demurred, "at least half the class never wanted anything else but to be on the Ship, and at least thirty of them got cut out. I think there's a certain amount of luck involved — "

"Luck!" Ching scoffed, "luck has nothing to do with it! We're here because, basically, we worked harder than the others at what it takes . . . "

"Compatibility, too," Teague said, "I think they tried mixing different combinations and we just came up as the ones who were most likely to be able to adjust . . . "

"I suspect," said Peake, "that we'll be debating that point for the next nine years or so! Why it was us, and not some other members of our class. But does it matter?" He yawned. "I'm tired. Excuse me — I want to explore the sleep cubicles. It's your on-shift in navigation, Ravi, if anything should come up — "

"It won't," Ravi said, "as far as I can imagine, we could probably get along without any of us going to the Bridge for the next nine years or so." His arm was still around Moira's waist. He made a small, interrogative sound, tightening his arm around her. For a moment she was abashed; there was a momentary silence in the cabin, and she felt as if everyone was looking at them where they sat. Then, defiantly, she tossed her head. In this crowded ship everybody was going to know what everybody else was doing, and she had no reason to be ashamed of it. She might as well start the way she intended to go on, doing what she chose.

I'm not like Ching, I can't be as self-sufficient as she is. I need people, I'm frightened. . . . The very thought of the vast window on the stars made her feel dizzy and weak, the steak curdling her stomach; she clutched at Ravi, hungry for reassurance.

Fontana said, "I think we all need a break. Suppose we all meet in four hours, here, for the first of those music sessions? Peake, you know Schubert's *Nocturne* for piano and violin, don't you?"

She knew he knew it, she knew it perfectly well, Peake thought angrily. She was rubbing it in. He and Jimson had played it at the last of the Academy concerts, they had been playing it that ghastly final night. . . . *Queers,* he heard again the taunt Jimson had flung at him. But Fontana was testing him, perhaps, seeing how well he could stick to the agreement not to cling to the past or torment one another with memories of those who were not with them. He said, "Sure, I know it, can you handle the piano part? I don't know how it will sound on an electronic keyboard, though."

"We'll try it, anyhow," Fontana said.

Teague said, a little diffidently, "Would anyone like to try the Mozart clarinet quintet?"

"I'll take the second violin for that," Ravi said, and they agreed to meet.

The six sleeping cubicles were arranged in a semi-circular pattern around the spherical module; each cubicle, Ching had expected, would be the shape of a section of tangerine, but instead the cubicle was

vaguely roomlike, the ends chopped off; she supposed
that was to make them feel familiar, safe, womblike. At
one side was a bunk with a restraining net; on the other,
a small cubbyhole with shower and washing equipment, this part heavily DeMagged to full gravity for
proper water-flow. She brushed her perfect teeth, feeling some comfort in the familiar ritual, and realized
she had forgotten to get herself a disposable nightgown,
or fresh clothing for the next shift, from the machine
in the hallway. Darting out for it, she saw Moira and
Ravi coming out of Moira's cubicle, turning into Ravi's,
and heard their husky laughter. She felt a sadness too
deep for mere envy. *What does she know that I don't
know?*

She punched the proper co-ordinates for fresh disposable clothing, stuffed everything she was wearing,
except her panties, into the recycling chute. She had
no particular modesty taboos, but somehow she could
not force herself to strip to the skin before Moira and
Ravi, who were behind her, also stripping, stuffing
clothing into the recycler, stark naked. She turned her
eyes shyly away from Ravi, who was strongly erect,
and hurried into her cubicle, sliding the door shut. She
fastened the restraining net over her bunk, turning the
DeMags to half gravity, and forced her thoughts to try
and float free. Fortunately the cubicles were completely
soundproof.

*Why should I wear a nightgown? There is no one
here, nor likely to be anyone here!* She pitched it
fiercely out of her bunk and watched it drifting in lazy
circles, trailing one sleeve, until finally, in the low gravity, it settled to the floor. Then she slept.

CHAPTER FIVE

"I've always wondered what it would be like to make love in free-fall," Fontana laughed, turning down the DeMag units almost to zero; the reflex action of the twist sent her into a gentle somersault, and when Teague pulled her toward the bunk, he overreacted and sent them crashing toward the opposite wall where they came to rest against the safety net guarding the door of the shower cubicle and its full gravity.

"What is that? Irresistible passion?" Fontana laughed, and the very reflex of the laughter sent them bouncing away from the bunk. Before long they were laughing so hard that Teague lay back, helpless, unable to do anything at all with her.

"So much for all the jokes about the delights of making love in free-fall," Teague said, making swimming motions in the air toward the stud on the DeMag unit.

"I still want to try it," Fontana murmured, but Teague said, laughing, "I like my women to stay in one place—not go bouncing across the room when I do *this* —" he demonstrated.

"You've given me a good reason," Fontana whispered, and put up her face to him.

Moira slept at his side, but Ravi lay awake staring at the ceiling of the bunk, his mind on the huge window from the Bridge, opening on the vastness of the stars. The face of the Night, the face of god, perhaps, the very Unknown itself, envisioned by the religious philosophers of my ancestors.

It's too much, how can a human mind envision it?

And, irrationally, he thought; *I envy Ching. She manages to face solitude without refuges like this.* He looked, tenderly and yet with great detachment, at Moira, clipped under the safety net, her hair floating loosely around her as she slept. He knew, if Moira did not, that his immediate response to her had been a refuge, an escape from a vastness too great to imagine.

And yet somehow I must manage to face it. I have wondered about the spiritual truths of the universe. When I can look into that enormity which represents the Face of God, then perhaps I shall be able to contemplate the nature of Truth, the nature of God, the nature of the Universe.

Peake had dozed only briefly, and returned to the main cabin, sorting music, tuning his violin. He would have to face it sooner or later, the thought of playing without Jimson at the piano. Fontana and Teague came in together, then Ching, in fresh disposable uniforms — Peake had not thought of that, and felt a little abashed at his own rumpled one. Perhaps they should make a habit of turning up in clean fresh clothing for their daily music session. It would give structure to the rhythms of the day. There would be so little to do, strictly speaking, that rigid structure might defend them against any chance of boredom and apathy setting in. Moira came in, getting out her cello and laying it against her knee.

"Give me an A, Peake," she said lazily, and he sounded it.

Ching tuned her viola. Teague began putting his clarinet together.

"I'm better with a flute," he warned. "I haven't

88   *Marion Zimmer Bradley*

worked with a clarinet for some time."

"Is there any reason you can't play a clarinet part on a flute?" Fontana wanted to know.

"Only the tone color," Teague said dryly, "and the range. Come to think of it, I do have an alto recorder, which has about the same range as the clarinet." He went to the shelf where the various woodwinds were stacked. Ravi came in, asking, "Do you want me to play second violin in this one?"

Peake said, "You can play first if you want to," but Ravi shook his head. "The first violin part is too hard for me. I'm not that good."

When they began to play, Peake realized that Ravi was not being modest, but telling the precise truth. He was not much more than competent, as they all were competent, having studied violin since kindergarten. Nevertheless, he *was* competent. Ching's playing was beautifully nuanced, unemotional — but then, baroque music was not *intended* to be emotional; Peake suspended judgment until he had heard her playing some romantic music. He wondered if, being a computer expert, she would play Mahler or Schönberg or Mendelssohn in that same technically-perfect, unemotional way.

Moira was almost a virtuoso; he quickly discovered that she was a match for him. Perhaps they could play some violin-and-cello duets — and he flinched away from the thought. Was he so quickly disloyal to Jimson? When they finished the quintet, and Teague put away his clarinet — he had played only the first movement with the recorder and switched to the clarinet, saying it was a more flexible instrument — Ching, Moira, and Teague, with Ravi playing his drums, began improvising on a jazz theme, and Peake went to sit and listen, saying that the audience was also a valid part of a musical experience.

He listened to Ravi, who was as much a virtuoso on drums as he had been undistinguished on the violin.

Jimson had loved to improvise, to take off on a theme and carry it to new heights where Peake could not follow him. . . .

To Fontana it was obvious what Peake was thinking; he had agreed not to speak of those left behind, but could anything keep them from brooding? She came over and sat down on the arm of his chair.

"Still brooding over Jimson, Peake?"

"I suppose it doesn't make sense," he said, defensively.

"Considering that, within five years, Jimson will probably be governing a Space Station, and the probability of our surviving five years hasn't even been computed yet, I wouldn't think it made much sense to worry about Jimson," she agreed.

"It's just — I never even thought about what would happen if we didn't both make it. I'm having to — to rearrange all my mental furniture." He added, defensively, "You can't expect me to — to change everything in my head overnight, just like that, just cut him right out of my life as if he'd never even lived!"

"Well," Fontana said, "I know the books say it's inevitable that you'll mourn over the death of a relationship. I guess we've simply got to let you mourn. But I suspect that's why they don't encourage us to have relationships like that."

Peake wondered how she had managed to say that without even a hint, in her voice, of *you should have known better*, but somehow she managed it, and it encouraged him to ask:

"Fontana, was it wrong of us to want to be together?"

"Wrong? How can I say? Unwise, certainly. They'd have separated you, anyway, after graduation. There was never even a fighting chance you could have made it together on to a Ship. A Ship's company can be as few as four people; it would put an unholy strain on the other two, if the first two were a committed couple. There has to be room for outside commitment — sharing, affection, caring, with *everybody* on the crew."

"Then why did they take me?" Peake flared, "since, unwise or not, I *was* committed?"

And suddenly Peake faced what he really felt. It was not parting from Jimson which had hurt too much. That parting had been inevitable, he had already known that, he had begun to suspect that the parting was already overdue.

"What hurts, is guilt," he mumbled, "guilt that I was the one to go and he was the one to stay."

And the memory still hurt, that moment when Jimson had flung it at him, *Do you think they're going to take a pair of queers?* Against that memory he said, still defensive, "Then why in hell would they take me? I'm not going to fit in much better than one half of a — of any committed couple. It's not as if I'd been the only homosexual in the Academy. There was Fly. And Duffy. And Janet."

Fontana shrugged. "What can I tell you? I don't think it made any difference, any more than I think they picked Moira because they needed a cello for the string quartet. Homosexuality is a legitimate lifestyle option — there are years when it's been a plus quality, when there was an all-male crew. . . . Survey Ship number seventy-two was all-male, and I think seventy-nine was all-female. There were a couple of other all-male crews, too. One year — I read this in psychology — there was a crew where the top seven just happened to be males, and they sent an all-male crew. Compulsive heterosexuality would have been pointless on a crew like that. No, with Jimson it was something else. He was — he was so damned *defensive* about it.

Do you remember Duffy? He made a point of bragging that he'd never had a woman and never would. There are professions where that lifestyle could be an asset. But not on this particular Ship."

"Then why did they take me?" Peake wondered, but Fontana had no answer. She said, "I don't know, Peake. Maybe they supposed you were flexible enough to adapt, to — to live and let live. Or thought, maybe that you were strong enough to live that way. I just don't know. But whatever they thought, they knew Jimson couldn't — and since even I knew that, I guess it's probably the best they could do."

Slowly, painfully, Peake nodded. In his deepest despair, it would never have occurred to him to call himself — far less someone he loved — queer. He had loved Jimson without reserve, had not hesitated to define himself, at least in relationship to Jimson, as homosexual. But he had never thought that he would be thus defining himself for all time, and certainly he had never guessed at the reservoir of self-hate that had led Jimson to fling that insult at him — or at their love. And self-hate, he realized, would be about the most dangerous trait possible aboard a Survey Ship.

"I guess I really knew that all along. Thanks, Fontana."

She shrugged that off. "I guess I'm crew shrink, at least by default, and I figured it might be healthier to talk about it now than waiting six months and digging it out like a festering sore." She stood up. "Listen, you sing bass, don't you?"

"I can, provided it doesn't go too far below a low G — I never flattered myself I could sing Boris Godunov," he said amiably, relieved at the change of subject. "Why?"

"There's a mass in five voices by Byrd that I'd like to try. Ravi has a good tenor, and Ching's voice is beau-

tiful, when she'll be bothered to sing at all. And I'd like to establish the principle of equal time for vocalists around here. Listen," she said, raising her voice to include them all, "tomorrow, when we get together, can we try the *Byrd Mass in Five Voices?*"

"Fine," Teague said. "The music's in the computer, isn't it?"

"I'll play continuo," Moira said, "I don't sing. I'll play cello continuo, or piano — I mean keyboard — or turn the music, or sit and be an appreciative audience. But I don't sing."

"Why not?" Ravi demanded.

"Because female tenors, in general, sound considerably less attractive than male sopranos — which probably isn't fair, but happens to be a cultural fact. And I have a range of half an octave, all in the tenor register," Moira said, loosening the strings of her bow, and storing it in the case. She slid it over toward the wall, then turned and asked, "I suppose we're going to keep full gravity in here?"

"I don't see any objection," Teague said, "but there are going to be parts of the ship where we can't; I think we all ought to get into the habit of securing everything as if we were going to be in free-fall. Then we'll never have to stop and ask ourselves whether we have to."

"I don't think that makes much sense," Ching objected, but she stowed her viola in the racks and fastened the net over it. Fontana, helping Moira with hers, scoffed, "I don't believe a word of all that stuff about your voice, Moira. How did you manage to get through sight-singing class when we were all twelve years old?"

"Faked it," Moira said curtly, "sang falsetto."

Ravi leaned over her, lightly touching her hair. He said softly, "With a male soprano, one might be in — in some legitimate doubt about his fundamental nature, or the validity of his — shall we say, vital equipment?

It doesn't seem fair, does it, that a low voice in a woman should be the complete embodiment of sensuality — like yours."

"That's a common mistake," said Fontana, and for a moment Ravi was irritated — his words had been addressed to Moira, not a part of the common discussion. Then long training and natural good nature triumphed, and he said, smiling, "I'm probably sensitive on the subject; my voice changed late and as a tenor my virility was in doubt until I was fifteen or so — I don't mean from the medics, only from the others in the class."

Moira said, with a chuckle which reached only his ears, "You certainly have made up for lost time, haven't you, darling?"

Peake, who had heard Ravi's words but not Moira's, said, carefully securing a net around his violin, "There was a countertenor who gave a concert in Sydney; Jimson and I had permission to fly in and hear him; it was the same week Zora left us. He had a voice which was pure soprano — higher than yours, Fontana. And he was a big, blonde, hairy-chested man, and we heard that he was married with five children or so — came from one of the thinly populated enclaves. Iceland, somewhere like that." After he had spoken, he realized that for the first time he could remember, he had spoken Jimson's name without even a momentary twinge of that despairing guilt.

Had Fontana lanced that wound? Or was there some mystical awareness of the space, the enormous and widening distance between them, which made it, suddenly, seem as if Jimson were someone he had known a long time ago . . . ? Peake was not sure; he felt a twinge of regret at his own fickleness, but he recognized that as mere self-pity and grinned.

He said, "Music is hungry work. Seems to me it's dinner-time again, and then I'm going up to the Bridge to check instruments."

It occurred to Fontana that if this kind of musical session were scheduled regularly after a sleep period, it would painlessly evolve into the kind of daily shared meal that had been suggested; but she didn't say so, taking her small tray of food from the console and going to sit beside Teague. Ravi had settled down beside Moira, and Fontana, studying the pattern they made — the two couples, the two outsiders, Peake at one end, Ching beside the food console, studying the controls absent-mindedly as she ate — found herself wondering. There was no reason she and Teague, Ravi and Moira, should not have paired off that way, as they had done during the sleep period just past. But it did accentuate the separateness of the others. Like many women who come into contact with homosexuals, she wondered if it was amenable to change, if she would be the one who might possibly inspire him to change. Peake was attractive, certainly, with that graceful and rather endearing awkwardness, his surgeon's hands, solid with muscle and as steady on the violin as they would have been with a scalpel. Of course, Fontana thought, the ideal solution would be if he would pair off with Ching. But somehow she couldn't see it happening. Ching was too defensively self-sufficient. Any attempt to pair her off with Peake, simply because they were the two unattached crew-members, would certainly touch off that defensiveness, and make things worse.

Well, whatever their social patterns might be now, Fontana thought, they were sure to change within a few months or years; the six of them were going to be isolated for — at least — eight years, and there would be plenty of room for change, growth, experiment. She was fond of Teague, she had enjoyed giving him pleasure, but if he eventually moved on to one of the other women, she wouldn't object too much. Somehow she didn't think it very likely they would settle down as three monogamous couples, and it probably wouldn't be healthy if they did. The intensive study of small-group social and sexual patterns which had been part of her psychological training told her that what they felt for one another now was, through necessity, a transitory thing and subject to change and flow; but did the others see it that way?

Teague put his plate into the recycling machinery. He said, "Routine check, life support; I'll probably be doing it as a pure formality for years — I *hope* I will — but I'm going to check it every twelve hours, anyhow." He headed for the sphincter lock which led into the free-fall corridor between the main cabin and the module containing Life-Support controls. Ching and Moira followed and Teague noticed Ching inching along the crawl-bar, clinging tightly. His own impulse was to let go, push off, and go soaring the length of the corridor; Moira had already done so, but Teague pushed up toward the bar, behind Ching.

"Are you afraid of free-fall, Ching?"

Her head made a tight movement that he knew would have been a nod, except that her neck was locked tightly against the failure of familiar gravity. She said in a small voice, "Yes, I am. I think I might be able to get used to it, except that we keep having to go back inside gravity. . . . I never seem to settle down into one or the other."

"But you're going to have to learn to handle it," he urged gently. "Come on, trust me, I won't let you get hurt. Here —" he pried her hands softly from the rail, holding them in his own, and peripherally he noticed how very nicely shaped they were, and how soft and fine to touch. His arms were round her from behind, her slender body held against him. He said, "Relax, don't fight it," and, holding her, pushed off against the rail, not too hard, floating gently down the corridor. He curled round her, protectively; she made a soft moan of protest, and he felt her tauten into a fetal circle of panic, but they came softly to rest at the other end. She drew a sharp, shaking breath, and he said softly, "See? That didn't hurt you, did it? You could even get to like it, I should imagine — it's fun." He nuzzled his cheek against hers from behind, and said, "It's like lovemaking — the secret is to relax completely and let yourself fly!"

The moment he had said it, he knew it was a mistake; he had not intended a genuinely sexual allusion or gesture, but, feeling Ching go tense in his arms, he knew he had lost her. She said formally, "I suppose I will get used to it sooner or later. Thank you, Teague." The formal thanks somehow were worse than a protest, and when she freed herself from his arms, he knew she had never really been there at all. She slid through the sphincter, clinging tight against the new orientation of "up" and "down," and lowered herself carefully to the floor. "I'm going through to the Bridge and check the computer," she said, and wriggled through the sphincter at the far end, leaving Teague staring at his Life-Support consoles, frowning.

Well, I made a damn fool of myself, I might as well have saved myself the trouble.

But he put it aside to check the controls meticulously, then began thinking, again, about the pattern for his string quartet. He could compose a part of it on the computer, which would make an instant playback and printout of what he had written; but he supposed he would do a part of it, at least, the old-fashioned way, with music paper and stylus. Maybe he would do it all that way, not using the computer at all. Why not? He had plenty of time.

CHAPTER SIX

Later that day they passed through the orbit of Mars; the planet itself was far off on the other side of the sun, and they did not see it. The course they had set was far off the plane of the ecliptic; Peake double-checked it, with morbid care. At their present acceleration, coming too close to the asteroids could be fatal; even the smallest planetesimal, encountered unexpectedly, could strike through a vulnerable section of the ship and create difficulties — if not disaster. Peake turned round, checking on the location of the pressure suits which were stored near the sphincter lock of the module — as they were in EVERY module, without exception — wondering if there would really be time to get into them if they were holed by a miniature asteroid. *Maybe. If it wasn't too big. If it didn't instantaneously destroy the module, crew and all.* Had any of the Survey Ships met this fate? He knew they would be monitored, on long-distance telescopes, at least to the orbit of Jupiter, and perhaps beyond. But once past the orbit of Pluto, they were out of range of any Earth-monitoring, until they reached the colonies . . . he turned to Moira, bent over the controls of her light-sails, and as if she could feel his glance, she raised her head and gaven him an uneasy smile.

He remembered that Moira was psychic; was she picking up on his fears? But after a moment he forgot it again, for she was bending over the machinery, crooning, it seemed, to the controls. They were all familiar with Moira's habit of talking to machinery, it was as much a part of their background as his own skill with the violin, or Zora's voice, or Teague's freckles.

Behind him Ravi said, and he was looking at Moira too, "She talks to them — the sails, I mean — like a mother to her starving baby."

Peake's mouth twitched. "She comes from one of the rich countries. Probably never saw starving babies," he said, but the picture was in his mind, clear, from his third or fourth year; he had come from one of the last enclaves on Earth where famine was still recurrent, and he had lived through one of them. So, he remembered, had Ravi.

"Why were we the lucky ones, I wonder?" he said to Ravi. "I was four years old, I remember, the baby died, seven babies in our village died, others never were the same . . . "

They had spoken of this before. Not often. Ravi, his mind filled with pictures of dark faces anxiously bent over dying children, said grimly, "I remember. The answer they give us at the Academy, that we were survivor types, brilliant enough to pass Academy tests, that never satisfied me somehow. We lived. So many died, and then we were taken out and pampered, given everything — how could we possibly have deserved it?" Ravi looked out at the panorama of the stars. He said, not really to Peake at all, "I can't believe it was the will of God that we should live and they should die, that God woud be concerned with anything that small, and oh, God, it looks so much smaller out here . . . " and he stared as if he could somehow wrench

an answer from the unyielding, endless points of light
out there.

Peake said, lapsing into a dialect long forgotten, "We
paying for it, man. With out lives. With losing everybody."

Ravi thought, *What shall it profit a man to gain the
whole world, if he lose his own soul.* . . and· he thought,
our souls have been taken from us by the Academy
training, and I am being sent where I have no chance
to find mine . . . and he remembered that a scant few
hours ago he had been blocking all of this out by frantic
sex with Moira. Somehow he would have to retrace his
steps, think about what and who he was . . . what had
Moira, and sex, to do with this struggle in his mind?
Or were he and Moira both a part of a Cosmic whole,
all part of God . . . he had read something of Tantra,
where the sexual partner was loved and worshipped
in the place of God. The idea, and the juxtaposition of
the two ideas, confused and annoyed him. He had been
brought up to be very casual and guilt-free about sex,
and now he wondered if this was simply a part of the
altogether soulless and atheistic Academy training.

Peake, at least, had not known casual sex, but a deep
and intense love. Perhaps Peake, at least, knew what
it was to love and revere a partner as if that partner
were a part of God. Like many strongly heterosexual
men, Ravi found it difficult to understand the impulse
which had brought Peake and Jimson together. He began, with a mental shyness strange to him, to think
about it. No one who had watched them together could
doubt that it was a stronger impulse than most of the
easy and casual heterosexuality in the Academy. It
showed most strongly when they were playing together, violin and piano; whatever was between them,
perhaps they had been able to achieve that ideal of

finding God in one another, without even the physical lure of opposite sexes.

I envy them, he thought, surprised at himself.

And then he began to think about Peake; the one of them who had known that kind of love, and the one of them who, because of what he was, was alone, with no chance of finding that kind of partnering again.

He will be alone, all during this voyage, and after having known a kind of love none of us has equalled.

Peake was one of them, and it occurred to Ravi, suddenly, to wonder if he could endure to see Peake completely alone all during this voyage. Did he and Teague have some kind of responsibility, since all of them were close as in — Moira had said it — one of these arranged marriages, to lessen Peake's loneliness?

I am his friend; his partner, even, in navigating the Ship. Could I, if he needed me, be his lover too? The thought scared Ravi a little, and he turned and looked surreptitiously at Peake, who was studying the vast view beyond the lenticular window.

"Doesn't it make you dizzy?" he asked.

Peake shook his head. "No," he said, "I like it."

Moira raised her head from studying the sails (a taut and twitching triangular corner against the stars), and said with a flick of sarcasm, "I am sure the Universe is happy at your approval."

Peake was too dark to display a blush, but he lowered his head with a sheepish grin, and Ravi felt a sudden deep tenderness. He knew, suddenly, that he loved Peake too, and whatever happened, he wasn't going to let him suffer in the years to come.

But he knew, too, that he was going to go on having sex with Moira just as long as she was in the mood!

During the next twenty-four hours, the crew explored the last corners of the Ship that they had not seen; the

modules controlling the light-drives and the sails, the
converter mechanisms which worked to recycle and re-
molecularize materials into food, clothing and the
other materials they needed for life abroad; although
only Teague, in a special radiation suit, went into the
main converter area. Moira explored the light-drives
which she had helped to assemble, remaining there so
long that Fontana became a little frightened and went
in after her. Ching refused to allow anyone else inside
the computer center under any conditions; she wore
anti-static clothing, and stayed in only a few minutes.

"Just long enough to get the general layout in my
mind, in case anything should go wrong — and let's
hope it won't — and I have to go in and actually do
something to the hardware," she said, coming out and
shucking the anti-static suit, "and I'm not giving any
conducted tours. Some time in the next year or two,
if anybody would like to learn what I know about computers, I'd be delighted to have a second-in-command-
of-computers, or a backup technician. But not until I'm
absolutely sure I know every inch of the thing myself!"
She stretched, cramped — the interior of the computer
module was somewhat smaller than she was, although
she was not very large. "Not you, Peake — you'd never
fit in there. You'd feel like that old torture — the box
where you can neither sit, stand, nor lie down! I'm
tempted to go and work out the kinks in the gym —
none of us has been in there yet!"

"Sounds like a good idea," Peake agreed. "Moira's
fussing around the sails again, but when she finishes,
we can all go."

They had to pass through two of the free-fall corri-
dors to get to the module tagged as a gymnasium.
Teague, who went through just behind them, noticed
that Ching's clinging to the crawl bar was a little less

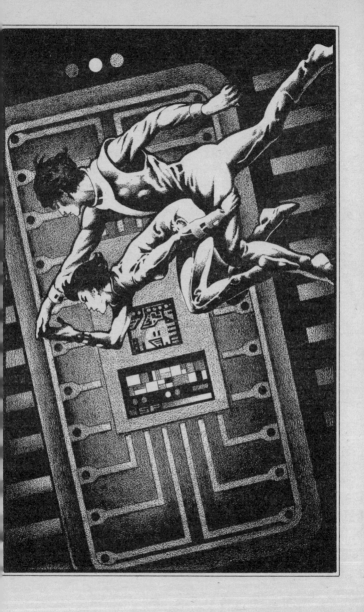

desperate, that for the last few seconds she actually let go and floated. So his efforts hadn't been entirely wasted, after all.

"How do you want me to set the DeMags?" he asked Peake, who was immediately behind them.

"Full gravity," Peake said, "at least for the first hour. One hour workout at full gravity, plus a four-hour sleep period at full gravity, will keep muscles and internal organs in tone. After that, if you want to experiment with low-gravity acrobatics, that's up to you. But as the medical officer, I make it a professional recommendation with all necessary force — no less than one hour of full-gravity exercise per crew member per twenty-four hour ship's day!"

"My, how solemn," Moira laughed, coming in behind him. "We ought to have chosen you for captain, Peake, you have the right accent and the proper authoritarian manner!"

"I'm a doctor," he replied. "This isn't an opinion, this is a medical necessity. Just a simple fact. Ignore it at your body's peril."

"Gravity set," Teague said, and went to an anchored rowing machine, where he sat down and began to pull against it with his powerful muscles. Fontana, standing at one edge of the cubical module, looked appreciatively at his bare shoulders, then began a slow jog around the room. After a few seconds, in spite of the fact that she was an extremely healthy young woman, she felt her heart pounding, let herself collapse for a moment to the floor.

Peake went and bent over her. "Trouble, Fontana?" He felt for her pulse and frowned.

"Tell me, did you sleep at full gravity last sleep period?"

Fontana felt the color rising in her cheeks, and looked

quickly, guiltily at Teague. They had kept the DeMag units just high enough to keep them from drifting apart as they made love; afterward they had slept in zero gravity, floating. She shook her head.

"Now you see why you have to," Peake said soberly. "It doesn't take the heart very long to adapt to zero-gravity, and the heart's like any other muscle, it gets lazy when it isn't working; the muscles in the human body were *made* to operate at one gee. You'll need to work out twice as long today, and don't try that again."

She stared at him rebelliously, but the thumping of her heart had frightened her. Could they really lose fitness so swiftly outside the familiar gravity of Earth? "All right," she said soberly, "I'll remember, Peake."

Peake nodded and went off to jog around the edge of the room, setting himself a hard, unrelenting pace. At one side, Ching was clinging to a ballet barre, doing smooth, fluid knee bends — Peake rummaged in a packrat memory for the word, *pliés*. During a lifetime of physical training, all of them had had introductory ballet exercises for fitness, and some of the women still used them as a training routine. Ravi was running too, on a treadmill. Peake ran on, feeling the pounding of his bare feet against the floor, enjoying the slow acceleration of his heartbeat. He was, he assessed himself mentally, in excellent condition. He intended to stay that way, though he supposed the novelty of doing exercises in the little gym module might wear off fairly soon.

As he ran around the small arena, recurrently, he passed Teague at the rowing machine, and about the fourth time he realized that he, too, was looking at the red-haired youngster's superb muscled physique. Not, especially, with desire; just, he became aware that he was noticing Teague, and it dismayed him, he hadn't looked at anyone that way in years. Not since he and Jimson — he cut off that thought in midair, knowing Fontana had been right; looking back was pointless, simply a way to torture himself.

No harm in looking, he told himself grimly as he pounded around the track. *Especially when that's all it can ever come to. Teague and Ravi are both woman-chasers. Which is just as well because neither of them is my type, or ever could be.*

He had never thought about anyone that way — not, anyhow, after adolescence — except Jimson.

But why not? Why was I different? He had read the theory that homosexuality or heterosexuality is firmly established by the age of two or three. When the practice is free of social stigma, as in the Academy, at least one out of every five or six men will be homosexual; and there had been four or five besides himself in their class. All but himself and Jimson had experimented with women, too; they had simply been too wrapped up in one another.

I don't know how I feel about women. I never bothered to find out. And then Peake, running, realized that this kind of thought was the sort of thing which hard exercise was intended to exorcise; wholly preoccupied with the body, awareness and morbid introspection left the mind. He sped up his running to sprint level, and thought dropped away; he was simply enjoying the feel of his body, his feet drumming the track, his heart pounding, the feel of sweat bursting from his body.

When it happened it was not the way he had always thought it would be if such a thing happened. First he felt his feet slip slightly, as if the floor had suddenly become tacky and his bare feet lost their traction. Then, since he was moving too swiftly to check himself, he felt himself slip loose and plummet, free of gravity, toward the far wall. *Intertia,* he thought, *an object keeps travelling in the same direction unless something happens to stop it.* . .he twisted as hard as he could to roll up in a ball, struck hard with one shoulder and slid along — no longer *down* — the wall. He looked around. Ching was floating, clinging with one hand to the ballet barre, looking suprised and panicky; the force of her kick had flung her into the air with nothing to bring her down again. Fontana, Ravi, and Moira were floating in midair, while Teague, still in the rowing machine, was staring in dismay as it wobbled under him.

Moira, with the skill of the free-fall-trained athlete, was already aware of what had happened, and making sturdy swimming motions down toward the DeMag unit.

"The gravity went off," she announced, superfluously. "You didn't set it properly, Teague."

"Yes I did," Teague objected, climbing out of the machine with some difficulty, "See, it's still turned full ON — one full gravity."

Fontana came and joined them. "Granted, I'm not quite the expert on DeMag technology that you are, Teague, I *do* know something about them, and a properly set DeMag doesn't go off that way. There's supposed to be a fail-safe device in them which lessens the gravity very slowly, to prevent just this kind of accident. Someone could have been hurt —"

Teague had already removed the panel over the unit and was peering into its interior. Fontana thought he looked very strange, as if he were swimming down toward it, his legs sticking straight up from inside the box. Moira shoved Fontana to one side and joined Teague there.

She said, "There's nothing wrong with the unit. Are you sure you set it properly, Teague?"

"Positive," he said, "and if I hadn't, it couldn't go off suddenly like that." He withdrew his head slowly from the box. "It's all tied into the central computer for Life Support, and when it lets go — and nothing is perfect — it's backed up so that the changes in gravity are very, very gradual. It doesn't matter so much when the gravity goes *off* — but suppose we'd all been in free-fall, doing acrobatics or something?" He pointed at Ching, still holding the barre. "Anyone who'd been in midair like *that* would have come down with an impact — one of us could have broken a leg, a kneecap, a shoulder — what's the matter, Moira?" he asked, for the red-headed woman had gone white, her freckles standing out like blots.

Her smile wavered. She said, "I — I'm not sure. It's like that other time — "

Teague looked grim. He said, "I think we treat Moira the way coal-miners used to treat their canaries —when the bird keels over, something's wrong even if the miner doesn't feel it yet. When Moira looks like this, we assume there's a real emergency. Ching, if it's something in the computer — " remembering that free-fall bothered her, he pushed up, floating, took her hands and gently steadied her as she lowered herself toward the floor.

He said softly, for her ears alone, "It's got to be in your mind, Ching. You're a G-N; your inner-ear channels are by definition perfect."

She said, shakily, "I think somehow the geneticists missed that one," and unexpectedly, vomited messily into the air.

"Let her alone," Peake said swiftly, "Get her down!"

Ching moaned, still retching, "There isn't any *down!*"

Peake came and took over, checking her pulse, wiping her face. The others, with varying expressions of

disgust and exasperation, were dodging drifting glob-
ules of vomit. Fontana — she too, Peake recalled, was
medically trained — came over to them, a dampened
towel in one hand.

She wiped Ching's face with it, gently. Ching was
still retching emptily and crying, but as Fontana
touched her she made a noticeable effort to control
herself.

"I'm all right. I'm sorry, I couldn't help it. Here,
Teague, did you need help?"

"There doesn't seem to be anything wrong with the
setup," Moira said, her hands caressing the DeMag
machinery. "It's perfect, nothing wrong with it."

Fontana said with asperity, "Maybe we all dreamed
it."

Moira's voice was impatient. "No, no, that's not what
I mean. I mean, since there's nothing wrong with the
functioning of the DeMag, whatever it is, it's got to be
in the computer tie-in."

"The DeMags are all programmed alike," said Ching,
holding herself down with one hand and peering into
the box. "If there's anything wrong with the way this
one's set, they'd all have been doing it. And they're all
fine."

"Everybody hang on tight," said Teague, "I'm going
to try something." He moved the stud on the DeMag
unit all the way toward the OFF position. Then, firmly,
he moved it again toward ON.

Ching felt herself slide toward the floor; the gym was,
reassuringly, right side up again, and her insides settled
into comfort. She made a face of disgust at her stained
tunic, splattered with vomit and half-digested meat and
salad.

Ravi said, "And this time it went on the way it was
supposed to; slowly and gradually, so that nobody

plunged down and sprained an ankle or anything."

Teague was scowling at the switch. He said, "I'd better go and check out everything in the Life-Support
module. And Ching, you check out everything in the
computer tie-ins — "

"It couldn't be the computer," she said positively,
but at Moira's glare, she said, "All right! All right! I'll
check every linkage! But do you mind if I clean up this
mess in here, and go and change my clothes first — and
have a shower?"

CHAPTER SEVEN

As she showered, Ching thought about that.

She had insisted on cleaning up the mess in the gymnasium unaided (it had rained to the floor in a smelly shower when the gravity came on) before going to clean herself. Now she stood under the shower and scrubbed fiercely, letting the hot water wash away disgust and filth, sudsing detergent vigorously through her short straight hair.

Was it all in her mind? Granted, she had not specialized in psychology and, in fact, considered it a sloppy and inexact science. But Teague was right; as a G-N, she should have had perfect inner-ear channels, and this sudden nausea was evidently some kind of failure. She found it both puzzling and frightening. She had had perfect health all her life, except for a broken finger when she was nine, and the occasional 24-hour-virus. Now her body had betrayed her, and done it in the most humiliating way possible. Well, not *quite*, she told herself with a touch of bleak humor. She could have wet herself, or her bowel sphincters could have failed her like that, in public; *that* would have been considerably worse!

But she expected herself to be perfect, had taken her perfect body's co-operation for granted — she had

never even had a cavity in a tooth! Feeling the comfort
of the hot shower, flooding down, blessedly down on
her, she felt a sudden surge of repeated panic, *if the
gravity suddenly went off in here, I'd drown,* and firmly
reminded herself not to be foolish. The DeMags were
backed up by all sorts of fail-safe systems. She wouldn't
drown before she could get the water turned off. Why
was she being such a fool?

She stepped out, air-dried and combed her hair, enjoying the feel of its cleanness, and slipped into a clean
tunic and panties, slid her feet into paper slippers. She
thought, *I had better go and check the computer tie-
ins. Though it can't be in computer. . .* and again she
felt the feeling of sudden, wavery panic.

*I'm supposed to have a perfect body, complete with
perfect inner-ear labyrinths. If my own body can go
back on me like this, can I trust the computer?*

Teague had gone to check on the DeMag and Life-
Support units, and Fontana, as his second, had gone
with him. Ravi, whose shift it was, had gone up to the
Bridge to make the routine check of course, chronometer time, and navigation instrument readings. Peake
and Moira, having nothing else to do, had remained in
the gym, Peake completing his running laps, and Moira
working on gymnastic equipment.

Peake completed the hundredth lap — which gave
him a day count of a two-mile run — and slid down,
folding his long legs, to watch Moira whirling herself
over the parallel bars. He thought; *if the gravity failed
when she's doing that, she'd break her neck!* and felt
himself shudder.

She saw him watching her and jumped down.

"You're practically good enough for the Olympics,"
he said, smiling.

She said, with her throaty chuckle, "Quite a lot of

us are. We train very hard, after all, and there are a lot
of high-mesomorph types in the Academy — short,
compact, muscular. It's one of the physical arrangements that goes with high intelligence. The other kind
is like you — long, scrawny, ectomorph. There's even
been some talk of entering a few of us. Only the question is, what country's team would we join? Australia?
The world would complain, if Australia had a gene-
pool like ours to dip into. Our own? Nobody's supposed
to know where we come from, and this would bring us
back into national politics again. So — no Olympic
stars from the Academy."

"What country would you have competed in, if you
had?" Peake asked, "Would you have liked to?"

She shrugged. "I sometimes think it would have been
nice. I do like the limelight. Only if I'd had *that* kind
of ambition, I'd hardly have made it in the Academy,
would I?" she said, answering the last question first.
"I don't think I ever knew your real name, did I, Peake?"

"David Akami," he said, "and I'm from South Africa.
And you —"

"Ellen Finlayson," she said, "and I was born in Scot-
land, or so they tell me — I don't remember, so it's
hearsay evidence, after all." She chuckled again. "Do
you mind if I turn the DeMags off again? I had some
training in free-fall when Teague and I installed the
drives, and I've always wanted to try free-fall acrobatics — I watched the telecast from the Lunar Dome the
last three Earth Days."

"Fine with me," Peake replied, and Moira turned off
the stud, feeling the gravity slowly, slowly go off; at
first they felt faintly light-headed, a brief flash of disorientation, then the exhilaration of floating. Moira
bounded up into midair, turning a rapid series of som-
ersaults, spinning on her own center like a top; came

to rest laughing and flushed, stretching back and turning on her own momentum, arms splayed out.

"I wonder why Ching got sick? There doesn't seem to be anything sickening about it," she said, "I actually *like* the sensation of weightlessness."

"Her inner-ear channels may not be as stable as yours."

"Oh, come," Moira scoffed, "she's a G-N."

"In that case," Peake said, "it's only a matter of acclimatization; she'll get used to it very quickly. Don't make fun of her, Moira."

"I wasn't making fun of her, Peake," Moira said soberly, "I felt sorry for her. She's always been so perfect and self-controlled. Maybe that's it — it scares her to be out of control, because that's just one of the givens of her life. Being perfect. Like a computer. Any G-N takes it for granted — being perfect, I mean. You, and I, and all the rest of us, have to live with the fact that we're just conglomerations of random genes; if we made it into the Academy, that means that we're the end product of natural selection. You, more than me, because in your country the weaker ones die out in famines and so forth. So we know, if we get this far, it's because we, or our ancestors, had some superior stuff inside us, body and brain. Ching doesn't have that to lean on — whatever there is that's superior about her, she knows it's just that some scientist tinkered around with her parents' germ plasm. No roots."

All this was true, Peake thought; but he was surprised that it should be the tough-minded Moira who said it. He had not thought her sensitive enough to be aware of that. He discovered that he was looking at Moira in a new way; she too could be sympathetic, where, always before, she had intimidated him a little.

She pulled him up beside her; he felt himself bounce

a little on the cushiony air. "As I remember, you're a fair acrobat yourself," she said. "Come on, let's try double-spins around a common center —"

Seizing her hands, spinning, Peake felt the curious sensation that the world, not himself, was spinning while he remained wholly stationary at the center of the module which was dancing, somersaulting around them; that the absolute center of the universe was located somewhere in the small, lessening space between Moira's curled body and his own as the module whirled round them as the whirling stars moved . . . at the end of a long spin they slowly came to rest, almost in each other's arms. Slowly, holding each other, they drifted down.

Moira had felt it too, as if the universe centered to the location in the narrowing space between their bodies; she was reluctant to break the contact.

Peake said, laughing, "You're good at that for a woman!"

"That's nonsense," she laughed, without rancor, "That's like saying, you play the violin pretty well for a man! Do you really think skill at acrobatics is gender-linked?"

He shook his head. "Women have a higher percentage of body fat to muscle; their center of gravity is lower," he said, "and so, in general, men are somewhat better athletes. Or at least, so I understood, as a medical man — I'm not claiming to be an expert on athletics. If women are men's equals in that field, I apologize — I spoke out of ignorance, Moira, not male chauvinism."

"Apology accepted," she said, giving him a little hug. Then, as he spontaneously returned it, she came to rest, perfectly still, her eyes meeting his, straightforward and clear.

"Do you want to go to bed with me? If you do, it's all right."

Shock flooded through Peake; he felt as if the bottom had dropped out of his universe, the centering closeness suddenly replaced by empty cold. That had never occurred to him, it had been the last thing on his mind. The split second of panic was followed by a split second of cynicism, *Maybe I ought to try it, find out what it's like* . . . but panic, emptiness, and shock were all drowned in a sudden, uncontrollable wave of hostility.

"What's the matter? Isn't Ravi enough for you? Or can't you live with the notion that there's one man in the universe who doesn't want you? At that, I suppose I'm the only male in the Academy you haven't slept with, and you want to round out the collection to completeness?"

Moira's face whitened at his fury, but she did not withdraw or drop her eyes. She said, shaking her head a little, her curly hair flying out on the soft currents of air in the room, "No, Peake. I'm not ashamed of liking sex, but that wasn't the idea. I just thought — I thought it might make you feel a little less alone, that's all."

And suddenly Peake was ashamed of himself. He had felt alone, most desperately alone, isolated and friendless, and then when one of his new family made an offer of ultimate sharing with him, he reacted like this! He liked Moira, he had been astonished at her sensitivity — in his experience, most women were tough realists, incapable of the kind of gentle sentiment men could display. But still . . . something inside him refused to take this kind of comfort quite as lightly as that, meaning no more to Moira than the hug she had given him, a purely physical kind of comfort. He wondered if that was all that sex meant to women.

He said, fumbling, "I'm sorry, Moira. I shouldn't have said that. I — I know you meant it kindly, and I — I really do appreciate it. Honestly. But I guess I'm just not — not ready for that. Not yet."

Another sleep period had come and gone, and Teague sat in the music room, music paper and a stylus before him, scribbling rapidly. Ching came and looked over his shoulder.

"What's that you're doing?" Her eyes on the line of music, she sang it slowly and correctly, in a sweet clear mezzo voice. "That's a lovely melody, Teague, but I don't recognize it. Is it something that isn't in the computer? Something by Delius, perhaps? It has that feel."

"I'm flattered," Teague said wryly.

"You wrote that?" She looked down at him in surprise and admiration. "But Teague, it's beautiful, I didn't know you composed music!"

"I don't, very often," he said, "only when an inspiration comes to me, I guess."

"A sonata?"

"String quartet, eventually," Teague confessed, "and don't tell everybody about it, Ching. They'd probably think it was foolish. Nobody composes music now, with the computer doing everything better —"

"No," Ching said, "that's foolish. There's no substitute for human knowledge."

"I'm surprised you would say that, Ching. Aren't you the one who thinks the computer is God? Why, your very existence — it was computer technology which created the modifications in human germ plasm making the G-Ns possible, wasn't it? One could say a computer was your real father, couldn't we?"

Ching giggled. She said, "That brings up the funniest picture in my mind. . ." and for the first time it occurred to Teague that Ching's completely plain, ordinary face, without a single feature one could notice or remember, seemed somehow pretty and individual when she was laughing like that. Not a single good feature or a bad one; but somehow her giggle was completely unlike any other one he had ever heard.

Then she sobered, and her voice, always a little tense and didactic, virtually wiped out the memory of that charming laugh. She said, "No, Teague, I don't idolize the computer. Less than any of you, maybe, because I know more about them and what they can and can't do. We have to rely on them, though, because the — universe is just too big. Remember what Ravi said about the mudfish and the Great Barrier Reef? The computer can only do what we order it to do, and only if we ask it in just exactly the right way. It's like that kid game we all used to play in kindergarten — *Simon says take three giant steps* — and you had all the rigamarole of saying *May I — Yes* — and if you missed a single *Simon Says*, or *May I*, you had to go back to the beginning and wipe everything out. A computer is like that kid's game. Anything, if you ask it exactly right, and nothing if you don't. And speaking of computers, Teague, I did check every single tie-in for the DeMags, and I couldn't find anything wrong. All I can think of is that somebody bumped against the stud, while we were all exercising, and turned it off, and I'd suggest a safety housing for it."

Teague frowned, leaning back and raising his eyes and his attention from the music paper in his lap. He said, "I can't imagine how it could have happened. If the control of the DeMag in there had been a pressure stud, yes, I could see it. But it's a dial that has to be twisted clockwise to go *on*, and counter-clockwise to go *off*, and it's not all that easy to turn; it could hardly

have been turned off by accident. Nor can I imagine
any one of us doing it without warning the others;
Peake could very easily have been killed, and if he
weren't such a fine natural athlete he *would* have been
killed. None of us is stupid enough, to say nothing of
malicious enough, to do such a thing as a practical joke.
So, eliminating accidental turning-off, or deliberate-
without-telling-anyone — which would mean that one
of us is a psychopath who didn't care if he or she killed
someone — it winds down to defect in the DeMag, or
fault in the computer tie-in. Now Fontana and I checked
out that DeMag unit and the control, right down to the
core, and it was in perfect condition."

Ching frowned, thinking hard. She could feel again,
in her belly, the sudden nausea and fear as the gravity
left her disoriented, hanging upside-down from a ballet
barre which, moments before, had been stable and
solid. She said, "Could there have been a short in the
electrical wiring of the control dial, Teague? That
would explain why it went off suddenly, and then came
back again when you turned it off and then on again."

"Maybe, but we didn't find any trace of it," Teague
said. "Fontana thought about that, of course; it was the
first thing that occurred to her. Electrical circuits *do*
short out, of course, but all the electrical circuits aboard
this ship are computer-controlled anyhow, and they'd
hardly short out without some record — I mean, not
the way a regular wired switch would do."

"No question of that," Moira said behind them, "Fontana and I checked every circuit and everything in the
DeMag machinery before we went to bed, and it's pur-
ring along as sweetly as any old pussycat. Speaking of
which, I wish we could have shipped a cat or two. I
like live things."

"There are plants enough in the conservatory,"

Teague said, "but there were all kinds of arguments against any pets. Starting with contamination of alien worlds, and ending with the psychological problems of becoming attached to them and suffering when they die, or inbreeding causing monsters after several generations of kittens. Not to mention that cats react very badly to free-fall; worse than any other animal. Their inner-ear channels are even more sensitive than the human ones. More so, because they can't react to visual cues the way humans can."

"Oh, plants — that's not what I mean by live things," Moira said, going to the rack where the musical instruments were kept and getting out her cello, and a little later, Fontana came in, carrying a printout of the *Mass in Five Voices.*

"Ching, you can have the soprano part if you'd rather, you've got the range — you can sing a top A, can't you?"

"I'd really rather do the contralto part, Fontana. I like harmony. You and Peake can share the honors for the melody."

"The mass is a little complicated. I thought we could start with something shorter. You know this, don't you?" She hummed the opening phrases of the *Ave Verum.* Teague took up the bass part, surreptitiously sliding the music paper on which he had been writing into his flute case. Suddenly Moira's cello began to drift upwards; Teague grabbed for a shower of floating papers.

"Oh, *damn!*" He grabbed at handfuls of papers. Ching struggled to control sickness again, clutching at the doorframe and closing her eyes as the room reeled around her. Moira grabbed the cello, manhandled it into its case and snapped it safely inside, then purposefully forced herself down toward the DeMag unit.

"Now, damn it, this is *not* funny," she said wrath-

fully, and Teague stared at her.

"Do you seriously believe anyone would do this to be funny, Moira? Besides, nobody was near the dial —"

"No, I don't," she said. "Peake is too serious about working in full gravity, and Ravi knows perfectly well how serious it would be; and the rest of us were all here watching each other. But I couldn't even find a short in the way it's wired in. It's got to be the computer, Ching."

"I don't know why you all blame the computer," she said crossly, her eyes still squeezed shut against compelling nausea. She would not lose her breakfast, she would NOT! "I checked every tie-in to the DeMags and the programming appears to be perfect! Most of it I did myself, and I don't make that kind of mistakes!"

"Well, try what you did before, Teague," Moira said, twisting the dial firmly to OFF and then to ON again. The cello case thumped over on its side; if the cello had not been in the case it would have been crushed. Ching came down with a bump and a small, smothered cry.

"It's evidently something in the control dials, then," Moira said, touching it gingerly as if probing a wound "I'll take one of the dials apart and see how it's put together and why it keeps doing that. First in the gym, then in here, and God knows where it will happen next! And it could have been really dangerous, too." She glanced at Ching and said, "You look shaky; do you want coffee, tea, a drink — something stronger?"

Fontana said, "Brandy. Call it medicinal," and went to the console, dialing herself a drink and a slightly stronger one for Ching. "No, drink it, Ching. I'm not a qualified doctor in the sense Peake is, but I have had medical training, and right now this is what you need."

Slowly, Ching sipped the sharp liquid, making a face of distaste.

"Ugh, I hate that stuff!"

But even so, Fontana noticed the color coming slowly back into her face as she sipped.

Peake and Ravi came into the main cabin, and, seeing Fontana and Ching drinking, went to get themselves hot drinks. Teague said, "Cocktail hour, huh?" and got himself one, too. He scrabbled the music paper together, carefully separating his own from the printout of the madrigals Fontana had brought, and slid them into the flute case again. Then he began to pass out the parts.

"Fontana, soprano. Ching, alto. Peake, tenor. Ravi, baritone. And I'll sing bass," he said. "Moira, are you going to play for us? Or shall we go to the gym first and work out?"

"No!" said Moira, sharply, automatically and without thinking. Then, hearing what she had said, she began to rationalize it.

"I think we ought to — to stay out of the gym until we know what's happened with the DeMags. It's the easiest place to get hurt or killed, and if one of them went off suddenly, again, it might be more dangerous this time . . ."

Her voice trailed off again.

Ravi protested, "Look, one of the first priorities aboard ship is to keep our physical fitness. With the gym closed —"

Peake said sharply, "Moira's psychic; have you forgotten how we found out she was psychic? We stay out of the gym until we find out what went wrong with the DeMags, and that's an order!"

Teague raised his head and glared. "Who appointed you Captain of this ship, Peake?"

"As the medical officer in charge of physical fitness and safety —" Peake began, but Fontana swiftly interposed. She said, "We'll check out the DeMags as soon as we can. Meanwhile, we're all here, and it's time for music and then for dinner, in that order. Let's talk about it later. Arguing on an empty stomach never gets anyone anywhere." She turned to Moira. "Give us an A, will you?"

Moira stroked a soft string on the cello. She frowned, wondering why the thought of going to the gym had evoked such immediate, unprompted panic. Was it really another of those sickening psychic flashes, coming from nowhere and infuriatingly vague? Or was it her awareness of some flaw in the DeMags, subliminal, so that she *knew*, subconsciously, what was wrong and wanted to keep people away from it until it came into her conscious mind and she could fix it? She scowled, damning her Wild Talent, wishing it more accessible and more easily tamed, or else non-existent. She listened as Fontana sang the opening phrase of the *Ave Verum* in her clear, beautifully trained soprano; heard Ching and Peake join in, Ravi and Teague joining with the bass line.

When they finished, Ravi said, "Does everyone know the Mozart setting of the *Ave Verum*?"

Ching replied by singing the opening line. The voices answered one another. . .

> *O dulcis. . . .*
> *O pie . . . .*
> *O Jesu, Fili Mariae. . .*

Ravi, singing softly with his ear tuned to the other voices, particularly Peake's clear tenor, thought how strange it was that five agnostics or atheists, and one secret mystic, without any noticeable religion, were singing this music dedicated to militant Christianity;

that the greatest of Western music had been poured out
into this religion which had tried so hard to conquer
the world. Maybe their only triumph had been their
music, their masses and hymns, the work of Bach especially, the great flood of praise poured out in song;
music that actually survived the faith for which it had
been written. "*Miserere mei,*" Ravi sang, softly, "*Miserere mei, Domine . . .*" and as the five voices melted
into the great cadenced *Amen,* he had a curious sense
of merging with all of them, more intense than the
merging in any act of love.

*This isn't religious music any more, no one cares
what the words mean . . . true body of our Lord, what
rubbish. . . . but the music itself creates a form of rev-
erence for everything. . . . is it a psychological trick, or
is music, by its very nature, a part of God?* He had
studied the writings of his namesake, the great Indian
musician, who had written once that he did not *invent*
the *ragas* that he played; that he simply listened for
them, in the meditative mode, and they were poured
through his instrument. Was this what was meant by
the old phrase, *The music of the Spheres?*

They began the *Mass for Five Voices;* Ravi, unfamiliar with the music and sight-singing his part, for a time
had to pay strict attention to what he was doing; but
through it, he had the curious sense that in this shared
music, they were pledging a common faith and merging
with one another in a way more important than any act
of love. Faith to what? To one another? To their common roots, to the Academy? To the Ship? To the cause
they served without knowing why, which was, when
you came right down to it, rather like religion; none of
them had ever questioned *why* space must be colonized, the Survey Ships sent out year after year. So that
they were priests of a strange religion of space. . . .

Priests? Or were they simply blind worshippers?

They finished the *Mass;* somebody suggested more music, but Peake shook his head.

"My throat's dry; I need something to eat and drink." He went to the food unit. Moira put away her cello again, knowing that she, too, should find something to eat. *My throat's dry and I haven't even been singing! What's wrong with me?*

She had been trained to strict rationality; bit by bit she checked out the possible causes of her unease. Was she worried about the DeMags? That was troublesome, yes, but after all, it was only machinery, and she could understand that; if there was someting wrong in the mechanism, surely it was only a matter of time before she, or Teague, or Fontana, could locate and correct it, and meanwhile they would stay out of the gym and observe every precaution, secure everything for free-fall — she noticed that Fontana had stored the music carefully in closed bins.

Had she eaten something that did not agree with her? No, her breakfast had consisted of vitamin-C syrup and flat cakes of rice meal, with hot bouillon. Nothing that could upset the digestion of a sickly infant, and she had always been almost boringly healthy. Was her menstrual period due? No, not that either, and she had never had trouble with it, anyhow. Why, then, did she stare with sickened disinterest at the sizzling chunk of meat on Fontana's plate, at Ching's heaped salad?

Ravi came and settled into a seat beside her. "Not eating, Moira? Can't I bring you something? A little clear tea?"

"That would be nice," she agreed, "but you don't have to wait on me, Ravi, I can get it for myself —"

"Here, I have it," Peake said, turning from the console with a cup in each hand, "I was getting some for myself anyway. Moira, what's wrong? It's my business if anyone's sick."

"I'm not *sick*," Moira said irritably, "I simply don't feel like eating!"

"Fontana was feeding Ching brandy; you look as if you could use a good stiff drink," Peake said, but he didn't pursue the matter. Whatever it was, it wasn't serious enough to justify rank-pulling, assuming he had it to pull. None of them did. Maybe Ching had been right all along, that one of them should have had authority to make decisions.

Moira sipped her tea, feeling the hot liquid loosen her dry throat, but the unease still lay within her, a cold lump. She could see Ravi's eyes fixed on her, solicitous and troubled. Damn all men, anyhow, you gave them access to your body, because you wanted it as much as they did, and they kept on thinking it made some difference, that they somehow had the right to possess your mind and soul too! Machines made more sense. They were what they were, no matter how you treated them, as long as you gave them the kind of care their physical and mechanical nature demanded. Why couldn't men be content with that? Ravi was nice, and fun, and charming, and a skilled and ardent lover, but she felt hemmed in by the closeness he demanded. Was that why she had offered herself to Peake, to demonstrate to Ravi that he had no first mortgage on her body and soul?

Even Ravi's Wild Talent was a simple one; a purely mechanical one, utilizing the latent calculating skill of the brain. Some educator once had surmised — and seemed to prove it, by teaching children believed to be mentally retarded — that reading was not a learned skill, but a brain function. Arithmetic was probably the same kind of thing. But precognition?

Fontana came and joined them. She said, "I heard you humming along with Ravi on the *Ave Verum*, Moira. Listen, there's nothing wrong with your voice, and no reason you shouldn't sing tenor if you want to; you have perfect pitch, and all you'd need to do would be work on your breathing. I have a feeling, though, that if you worked just a little to develop your range, you'd be a very fine contralto. Ching's not a contralto, she's a soprano without a high range."

"I can sing a high B-flat," Ching said defensively.

Fontana retorted, "When I was studying voice, I was told that almost all mezzo-sopranos are just timid sopranos!"

"And *I* was told," Ching said waspishly, "that sopranos are lazy people who think it's easier to sing the melody than to learn how to read music and sing the harmony!"

Moira chuckled. "Cut it out, you two. *I* was told that singers are temperamental people, which is why I stuck to the cello!"

"Just the same," Fontana said, coming back to her original thesis, "I could teach you to sing as well as either of us — any of us — if you'd be willing to work a little. Not right away, but keep it in mind."

But Moira was not listening. Her face had suddenly gone blank, staring into nowhere, her features so relaxed, so mask-like that Fontana recoiled; she hardly looked human. Peake made a startled movement in her direction; he had seen an epileptic, once, in the hospital where he trained, look like that a fraction of a second before a seizure.

Then Moira screamed, a shrill, almost soprano scream. And in the next moment, like an echo of that shriek, all six of them felt it, a sharp, shivering shock, and then every siren and alarm bell in the ship went off.

CHAPTER EIGHT

It was a clamoring, deafening cacophony; and twelve years of reflex training and safety drills took over, without need for conscious thought. Peake found himself struggling into a pressure suit, his helmet latched shut, even before Teague managed to move toward the dial that would cut off the sound. Moira, even as she clamped her helmet, looked reflexively toward the bin where her cello was stored. In the moment before the helmet cut off sound, and before she got the sound in the suit hooked on, Fontana heard Teague slam the control that closed bulkheads all over the ship, confining airloss to the module which had actually suffered injury.

But only after Teague had closed off the deafening clamor, and all helmets were latched shut, the sound system opening their voices once again to each other, did anyone speak to put into words what had happened.

"A meteor," Moira said, in shock. "We're struck, we're holed! But how could that be? We were so carefully programmed to be outside the asteroid belt — "

"We are," Ravi said, "but we wouldn't have to be anywhere near the asteroid belt. There are stray bits of flotsam everywhere in the universe; and a piece no

larger than a grain of sand, hitting at our velocity —
which, I now venture to remind you, is more thousands
of kilometers per second than I like to think about —
could do very substantial damage to any module it hit."
Only then did he think to ask, "Is everybody alive and
all right?"

One by one, with wavering voices, they confirmed
presence and well-being. Moira was thinking, in shock,
*So that's what I was scared about, that's why I
screamed before it hit us.* She let herself slide down
toward the floor. "I'm all right," she said sharply, to
Peake's concerned question, "just a — a little shaky."

"Whatever it was — " Teague heard his own voice
wobbling as if it belonged to someone else and he had
no connection with it, "it's not in here; the air is all
right and the module's integrity isn't breached." He
heard the technical language with dismay; he'd intended to say, *this particular cabin is still in one piece.*
Strange, how reflexes superseded thought. He checked
the tell-tales again and confirmed. "Air level in here,
normal. Helmets can be unlatched for the moment.
DeMags, as far as I can tell, intact, gravity normal."

Whatever had struck them, then, it was somewhere
else in the clustered modules of the Ship, and the first
order of business was to find out where, and how badly.

Peake said, "I don't suppose there's any possibility
that it's a false alarm, like the DeMags in the gym going
off — something that triggered the alarm system?"

"I wish I thought so," said Teague, but Moira, rising
to her feet, said, "Not a chance. Listen, I've got to get
to the Bridge — "

"You think the trouble's on the Bridge?" Fontana
asked, wondering if Moira's psychism was still oper-
ative.

"I don't know," she said, "But — the sails — they're

spread out to surround every one of the modules — "

Teague checked her firmly, with a gesture, as she headed toward the sphincter lock. "Nobody's going anywhere, Moira, until we've checked the integrity of the Life-Support system and I'm in charge of that." He wriggled through, pushed along the free-fall corridor between the main cabin and the living quarters. The cubicles stood open around the clothing-unit, a careless drip floating around the room in Moira's cubicle, a discarded nightgown floating in Ching's. But the air levels were normal, the gravity came on when he flipped the stud on the DeMag and evidently the living quarters were safe. He looked grimly at the pressure suits hanging flaccid by the doors of each cubicle, identical with the one he was wearing. He had never really understood why pressure suits had to be duplicated in *each* module. Now he knew. Any module that was holed gave you a margin, perhaps, of eight or ten seconds to get into a pressure suit. No time to fetch one from another self-contained module!

But why had they been holed at all, this far from the asteroid belt? Space debris was so thinly scattered, elsewhere, that the chances of a direct collision should logically be extremely minute.

Well, even the longest odds sometimes made a hit — in this case, an extremely direct hit. He didn't think for a moment that the alarms had been set off by any such elusive short in the wiring circuits as had set off the DeMags. No such luck. The chances against such a collision were, literally, astronomical. Yet there was the Ship and there was the fragment that had struck them, in the same place at the same time. And the results — sirens, bells, alarms, and damage *somewhere*. But so far, all six of the crew were intact; and mechanical damage could be located and repaired. Somehow.

He wriggled back through the air-corridor, in free-fall, letting go, pushing off, re-entering the main cabin where the others waited.

"Living quarters intact," he reported, not mentioning the water-source someone had left dripping; it was no time to fuss about trifles, but it could be messy if the DeMags were off, and he made a mental note to speak to Moira about it. But not till the present crisis was over.

"I'll explore the Bridge next — "

"No," Moira said sharply, "I'm coming to the Bridge. We might as well all come along and see what's happened. I might be needed. Don't argue, Teague, you know I'm right."

It wasn't worth arguing about. And perhaps they should all stay together until they knew exactly what was happening. He opened the bulkhead leading into the other free-fall corridor, and checked. There was no rush which would have indicated vacuum, open to space, on the other side; no explosive decompression in here, anyway. Nevertheless, he ordered helmets latched before they all followed him into the corridor. Gravity was normal here too — meaning that there wasn't any. He pushed himself off down the corridor, the others following one by one; only Ching clung to the crawl bar, inching along, and for once they all waited for her without comment.

Peake was thinking about the hundreds of little blinking lights lining the control panels on the Bridge, reflected in the great lenticular window on the universe. In his mind was a terrifying picture of that window shattered and open to space, of the little lights extinguished, of themselves falling, falling, accelerating forever into the nowhere of the stars . . . his whole body felt clenched, taut, and when he thrust the pres-

sure-suit against the sphincter lock into the Bridge
module, he could feel the fresh spurt of adrenalin like
a cramp in his calves, a tingle in hands and feet. He
was the first into the Bridge module, and it was like a
wave of sickness, the sickness of pure relief, as he saw
the window undamaged, the blinking lights of the controls unchanged except for the great red wavering glow
of the ALERT tell-tales.

"Bridge module undamaged," he said, tersely. "Air
normal."

"My shift," Ravi said, unlatching his helmet and slip-
ping into the seat. Ching said, "I can check the tell-
tales from here. Life Support control module unbreached. Air levels normal. Drive mechanism module,
unbreached; air levels minimal, controls undamaged."

Ravi said, frowning at the course readouts, "This isn't
the course I set."

Teague, checking the readouts a fraction of a second
behind Ching, said, "Oh-oh. Here it is. Gym; red light
for explosive decompression. Whatever it is went
straight through the gym; someone will have to go and
find out what hit us, and how much damage there is."
He looked at Moira with a sudden gasp of wild surmise.
She had known.

"Could hardly be better," Peake said. "Nothing much
in there except empty space — "

"There's space in there now, anyway," Ravi said,
"hard vacuum."

"Well, if something had to hit us, that's the place
where it would do least damage," Peake said. "If it had
hit the living quarters, we could have lost a lot; or the
main cabin, holed, could have wiped out the musical
instruments, anyhow. And if it had hit the computer
module — I don't even want to think about that!" They
were all breathing harder now, with the relaxation of

tension and fear. The crisis was over; the damage was manageable.

"Someone will have to go in, in a pressure suit, repair the damage, reseal it, but there's no hurry," Peake said. "We do have to get some exercise, meanwhile, but if we have to, we can set the DeMags to two gravities in the living quarters and do isometrics."

Moira was not listening to him. She cried out, as if in agony. "Oh, no!" It felt as if the damage were in her own body, as she saw the great translucent sail wheeling across the stars outside the cabin. Where it had been firm, pressured tautly to the source of the light, now it streamed in tatters, trailing away behind the module and out of sight. It was a physical pain, seeing the proud sail dragging out in shreds and wisps of disintegrating film; she could almost *feel* the impact, the slicing pain . . . . She stared at the sail remnants, in dismay, and began to cry.

"Of all the damn silly things to cry over!" Teague said impatiently. "We have spare sails, and if we didn't, we could synthesize them!"

"It's not that," Moira said, sniffing. "But — they were so beautiful, and — and look at them — "

"Let her alone, Teague," Fontana said. "It's the strain. It's all right to cry, Moira, you can cry if you want to."

But Ching, following Moira's glance, felt tears in her own eyes. She knew precisely how Moira felt. *She may not think I'm capable of understanding, but I do. You can trust machinery, it's the one thing you can always trust, it's supposed to be perfect and it is, it's the one thing you can always be sure of being just exactly what it is supposed to be. And this — it's like rape, a violation, something intruding into an area you thought safe, personal, protected.*

She put her arm around Moira's waist; dimly she

remembered rebuffing some such gesture from Moira, some time ago — but Moira did not pull away from her, and Fontana wondered if she had ever heard Ching's brisk voice so gentle.

"The thing to do, Moira, is to get them in, if you can do it without further damage, and try to get another sail out; we could veer off course if the sails aren't properly trimmed for the drives. But the extent of the damage will be recorded in the computer, and any deviation from the set course; I'm going to check that, right now. Do you want some help getting the sails in, or would you rather do it yourself?"

Moira's in shock, Fontana thought; *and Ching's doing what I ought to be doing. Who would ever have thought Ching could function as a psychologist?*

Moira said, "I think I — I'd rather do it myself." She knew it was absurd; but somehow she had the feeling that her own gentle hands on the sails would damage them less than another's. She was still capable of being surprised at her own reaction, knowing it to be completely irrational. *It's as if Ching really understood. But how could she?*

Ching patted her shoulder, said, "If you need any help, Moira, I'm here."

Ching watched Moira for a few moments before going to her own console, but Moira's thin freckled fingers seemed perfectly steady on the control sails and she could see, out the great window, the movement of the torn sails as they began to reel inward. She said, "Shall I check any deviation from course, Ravi?"

He nodded, frowning, taut. He said, "Deviation or no deviation, we are *not* on the course that I set. Peake, did you change anything when you were on duty?"

Peake shook his head. "No, not at all."

"That's foolish," Ching said, frowning at her console,

"if it's the course you fed into the Navigation controls and then into the computer, it's the course we're on. There could have been some small deviation from course when we were struck — I'm going to check that right now — "

"But if we were struck hard enough to knock us that far off course, there would be a great deal more damage," said Ravi, and his voice was stubborn.

Ching frowned at the smooth, luminous figures that came up on the readout. "Did you alter the course at all after Peake formally laid it in? When you do, you ought to enter it formally into the log, and let us know. Because there is a deviation here, more than the sail damage could possibly account for, and I don't see any course changes recorded."

Ravi shook his head vehemently. "I didn't," he said. "When I first took over from Peake I saw a small deviation from the course he had set, and I corrected for that deviation, so that we're back on the original course, or should have been. But according to this — " he waved an unsteady hand at the readouts, "we're not anywhere near where we ought to be. We're some hundreds of thousands of kilometers closer to the plane of the ecliptic than we ought to be, though I wouldn't have thought we were close enough to hit the fringes of the asteroid belt."

Ching touched her console for a position reading, and stared, disbelieving; painstakingly went through the sequence again.

"That's not where we are," she said positively.

"It certainly isn't where we're supposed to be," Ravi agreed. "Even by dead reckoning I can make it closer than that, if we're still aiming at the T-5 cluster as we agreed. Jupiter isn't where it ought to be, compared to our position. Just look."

He pointed. They could all see the great planet, but only Teague, regarding it with an astronomer's interest, paid any attention. Ravi's fingers raced on his own console, and at last he said formally, "Please read out your figures, Ching, because that's not at all what I make it."

Ching read out her answer from the console, and at Ravi's frown she touched buttons to re-set and re-calculate position and course. This time they could all see the differences.

"But that's not what I got the first time," Peake said, "and that's what I put into the course calculator. Why is it different?"

"Now wait just a minute," Ching said, "if that's what you put into the calculator, that's what you got out of it. A computer gives only one answer to the same question. That's why they have them. The whole point of a mathematical calculator — and that's what you're doing with the computer right now — is to eliminate human errors in arithmetic. It's not like the story they told us in kindergarten, about the little boy who was asked if he had checked his homework — "

"Sure. I checked it three times. Here are the three answers," Ravi quoted, with the contempt of the person to whom mathematics is a natural language, making more sense than any other language; who could no more add a set of figures wrongly, or use the wrong equation, than the natural grammarian could split an infinitive. "But just the same, that's what I make it, and that's what the computer makes it, and there isn't any congruence between them. Peake got something else — "

"And I tell you again," Ching said, really angry now, "that computers don't make mistakes. Only the people programming them make mistakes. And in this case I didn't make any mistakes, because you saw me enter

the figures exactly as you gave them to me."

"Ching, there's no need to get angry with me," Ravi said, "I'm not attacking your competence, or your personal integrity, or anything of that sort. Computers may not make mistakes, but they do have mechanical failures, don't they? And programmers do make mistakes, and you didn't program this one entirely by yourself, did you?"

She shook her head. "Most of the information in the library was put in storage at Lunar Dome," she said, and clenched her fists, fighting a surge of anger and fear. Somewhere outside herself she knew that Ravi was not attacking her, that it was irrational to feel so threatened. Yet she did feel that it was her own integrity that had been questioned, not that of the computer.

I can't trust my own body. I can't trust the computer. Is there anything left that I can trust?

Defiantly, she pressed the console again for *re-set and re-calculate.* This time they could all see it; a third set of figures like neither Ravi's nor her own, flower in liquid-crystal numerics across the console. Fighting panic, Ching erased the figures and this time, painstakingly, she entered the relevant figures for the known position of the T-5 cluster, the position of Colony Six, and the elapsed time since departing from the Space Station. Her fingers pressed hard against her mouth as she watched the fourth set of figures flowing across the readout screen.

"What does it mean?" Fontana asked. "Does it mean we're on the wrong course? Or did whatever hit us damage the computer?"

"No," Ching said, and her voice was shaking too, "there's no damage to the computer module; I'm as sure as that as — as I can be of anything. But there's something wrong with it. I'm not sure yet just what it is.

What I am sure of is that it's giving us wrong answers. Lots of wrong answers. Everyone here is getting different information out of it."

Silence; and six stricken faces on the Bridge. None of them had to put it into words. Every one of them knew that without accurate information from the computer, they were all hopelessly lost, adrift among the stars without accurate data enough to know where they were going, or even where they were.

It was Fontana who first put the question in all their minds:

"Can it be fixed?"

Ching struggled against her growing fears — fear that she would lose control, somehow do or say the wrong thing. She said, slowly and precisely, "A computer is a machine; we can do everything the computer does, only not quite so quickly or so well. And once I can find what is wrong with it — mechanical damage, a mistake in the original programming, once we know precisely what is wrong, it can be repaired. Repaired, that is, if the damage is mechanical; re-programmed, if it's a case of human error. We are particularly fortunate to have Ravi with us, because he can be used to check the accuracy of the computer. That's not the problem. The problem is — " and she swallowed hard, trying to steady the shameful terror in her voice, "that all during the time we're trying to find out what's wrong, and trying to fix it, we're still accelerating at a steady one gee — that means nine point eight meters per second per second — piled on to whatever velocity we've attained in the past two-and-a-half days. And every second we use to get it fixed, we're going further and further off course! An error of a thousandth of a degree in course might not make any difference at all on the surface of the Earth; because there's only twenty-four thousand miles you can go, and you're right back where you started. But out there — "Ching made a numb gesture at the infinity of stars beyond the observation window, and clutched at her seat, feeling as sick and dizzy as if the gravity had somehow gone off and she was falling endlessly through space, "out there, a thousandth of a degree here can get us *millions* of kilometers, light-years off course at the other end . . . . We may never reach the T-5 cluster at all, we may never reach *anyplace* humans have gone before! We don't know if Peake ever laid in the right course at all, or where we're going, or where we've been . . . it's probably too late to get back on the right course, even if we could find out, now, what course we *should* have taken from just outside the Space Station! We're going out into the unknown whether we want to or not — and we don't know where!"

CHAPTER NINE

In the silence following Ching's outburst, the sails rotated, slightly, so that they could all see the transparent shimmer of the film across the observation window; behind them the stars blurred. *All sails set,* Peake thought, *and acclerating at full speed — to nowhere!*

Ravi said calmly, "It can't possibly be as bad as that, Ching. We have a known position for the colonies and for the T-5 cluster, and fixes for most of the known stars. Surely, once the computer is working properly again, we can find out exactly where we are, compared to where we ought to be, and reset a proper course to take us there. The ship is maneuverable, after all, it's not as it was in the old days of the unmanned probes, where once set in orbit, the probe continued until it either crashed into something, or fell apart. We can maneuver fairly well; if we absolutely had to, we could cut acceleration, coast to rest inside the orbit of Pluto until we knew exactly where we were and in what direction we had to leave the Solar System, and then restart the drives. Theoretically, we could even turn ship 180° and decelerate back in the direction we came, to the point of the original error."

Peake made a small weak sound, almost a giggle.

He said, "I can hear it now. We slide into orbit alongside the Space Station. They say, hey, what, back already? We told you not to come back till you found us a habitable planet. And we say, sorry, folks, the computer you gave us doesn't work. . ."

Moira made a small finicky adjustment to the replaced sails. She reminded herself of a woman pulling herself together after a rape, trying to reassure herself that she is still alive, still essentially undamaged, still able to function. She tried to recapture the ecstatic sensation of being at the center of a great web, controlling the movement of the ship, controlling the flow of the universe — it would not come. All she felt was the shaking of her own hands on the controls; the one thing that was real to her, the perfection of machinery, solid and without human fragility and limitations, had been breached. She looked at the sail blurring the stars and thought of the thickness of it, measured in micrometers. How frail and frangible it seemed, shivering in the vacuum, cold against space as she was cold in the heated cabin.

Teague was looking at the great disk of Jupiter, and regretting the lack of the stability of a planet to take any sort of standard observation. He knew Jupiter's position in the Solar System, but he did not know precisely where the Ship was and that meant that he had no way of knowing precisely where anything else was, relative to it. But he said, "We have an absolute set of locators out there; Jupiter and its moons. We can find out precisely where they are and where they ought to be at this moment in Universal Time —" he gestured at the cumbersome True Time figures still streaming, with relentless, pulsing precision across the room of the cabin. "Even if we had lost all the cosmic data in the computer, we could re-calculate it all from the position of Jupiter and the Sun."

The Sun's disk, very far away, very dim and pale and
only a blot against the stars, at a far corner of the lenticular window, seemed incredibly distant. Suddenly
there was the loud clanging of an alarm; they all
jumped, and Fontana gasped as the red pulse of an
alarm-light flicked on and off.

Moira's hands were already moving, trimming sails.
She said, "I've got it; just a proximity alarm; a hunk of
debris." She reached to cut off the sound, the vibrating
red carbuncle of the emergency light. "Wherever we
are, I don't like it here and I suggest we change course
enough to get well out of the plane of the asteroids. We
aren't maneuverable enough to run the gauntlet of the
asteroid belt."

Ching, by automatic reaction, touched the computer
console, and stopped dead, her hands frozen. She said
weakly, "That's no good, Teague. You know where we
are in reference to the asteroid belt and Jupiter —"

"I can get us well off the plane of the ecliptic, and
that'll keep us away from most asteroids," Ravi said,
"but Ching, you've got to do something about the computer as fast as you can. How long will it take you to
check it out?"

"There are a few things I can do right away," Ching
said, "I can probably have some idea of what's wrong
inside a few minutes." She touched a few buttons,
frowned at the results, repeated the process. Then she
whistled, a small, sharp sound.

"Peake," she said, "enter the course you laid. Let me
watch you do it."

Slowly, meticulously, rechecking it with the tiny
calculator which was part of every navigation student's
permanent equipment, as much a part of him as his
head, Peake found the figures and ran them into the
computer. Ching watched, frowning a little.

"Now you, Ravi. Show me exactly what you did."

Frowning, Ravi complied.

"All right," Ching said, "I know what's wrong. Or — wait," she qualified, as five faces turned to her in expectant hope, "I'm not sure whether there are mechanical bugs in the computer itself; I'll have to get in there and find out. I'd have to do that, anyhow, to find out what's wrong with the DeMags, if Teague and Moira are sure there's no mechanical problem in them. But I know how we can get, at least, mathematical right answers out of the computer, because I know why it's giving us wrong answers. Ravi, are you aware that when you were converting the acceleration factor into days, you divided everything by twenty-four instead of twenty-four point zero?"

"As a mathematician," Ravi said, offended, "in a simple arithmetical function, there is no difference whatever between twenty-four and twenty-four point zero."

"Quite right," Ching agreed, "in a simple arithmetical calculation, and that's why the answer the computer gave you was wrong and you *knew* it was wrong. It's as if you'd asked it how long it would take to get to the orbit of Pluto at one gee acceleration and come up with a figure of eleven hours — utter nonsense that any mathematic idiot could spot. Or getting a figure of eighteen kilometers for the diameter of Mars. Only when the figures are astronomical, it's not so easy to check them. Normally, the computer — no, never mind, we stipulated that none of you has any computer sense. But I'll have to explain this so that we can get right answers out of it."

She frowned, fumbling for words which would explain to them something which was transparently obvious to her, now that she saw what had happened, but which would be as obscure to them as some of Peake's medical textbooks were to her. Finally she said, "I feel like a fool; Ravi's the mathematician, and it would be insulting his intelligence to suggest he didn't know the difference between a real number and an integer. But to the computer there's a tremendous difference — they're stored in a totally different format, and a real number is stored in twice as much space as an integer. Normally, the computer will convert all the integers to real numbers when they're used in arithmetic with real numbers, but now there seems to be something wrong with the Float subroutine, which should be doing that. So when the computer goes to do arithmetic, thinking it's using a real number, it picks up the integer and whatever is in the storage space next to it — giving results that can only be described as "unpredictable." Which means that even if you add two and two, you're likely to come up with five or sixteen, and when you get into complicated mathematical calculations, you have very serious difficulties. All right; we can still get the right answers from this thing —" she touched the console, frowning, "as long as we are very careful to float everything before we input it — in other words, don't put in any number, not even an exponent, without a decimal point. Or we could try putting everything in a binary —"

"Not on your life," said Moira with a shudder.

"Binary is as simple as our normal decimal system, once you get used to it —"

"But I don't have time to get used to it just now," Moira said.

Ching nodded. "In any case, we should still be able to get the right answers — assuming that we input everything as a real number, and assuming that the Float subroutine is the only thing malfunctioning — but we still shouldn't trust the computer until I have a chance to check everything out. And that includes programs already built into the computer as well as the ones we're putting in ourselves."

Moira asked soberly, "Is there any possibility that the meteor damage was to the computer module?"

They could all, Fontana thought, see the implications of that. Mathematical computations for the navigation, after all, could be done with the aid of their calculators, checked by Ravi's talent. But the computer was literally in charge of every other function of the ship. Gravity. Life Support. They were still running on stored food, but soon they would begin molecular synthesis of every mouthful they ate. Teague could see it too; he said wryly, "No chance the life-support computer tie-ins are screwed up? All we need is for the computer to start synthesizing H_2SO_4 instead of H_2O!"

Fontana shuddered. Ching said soberly, "I can't entirely exclude that possibility. I'll get inside the module as fast as I can, and check every unit inside it. No, I don't think there was damage to the computer module; the tests showed the integrity of the module undamaged. But even if it wasn't holed, we can't rule out secondary impact shock as a possibility. Or — considering that the first failure of the DeMags was before the impact — the possibility of some defect in programming, or some damage inside to the storage apparatus." She stood up and stretched nervously. "Crisis over. Just make sure I okay every figure you enter in the computer before you put it in. Ravi, do you know where we are?"

He bit his lip. "I will, before long," he said, "I'm getting a fix on Jupiter and three of the moons, and triangulating with the Sun; fairly soon I'll know our exact position relative to where we ought to be. Whether we can get back there without running the gauntlet of the asteroid belt, that's another thing; we may have made a critical mistake before we crossed the orbit of Mars, and it's just possible that the whole asteroid belt is between us and the direction we had intended to go. And unless Ching says the computer is back to where we can rely on it absolutely, I don't think we ought to make any major course corrections. There might be some kind of glitch in the mechanism which regulates the drives, so that we enter into the computer exactly what we want the Ship to do, and how we want to maneuver, and instead the Ship does something else."

He could see Moira shudder, and she lifted her hands from the sail controls and stared at them curiously, in a helpless way that seemed wholly at odds with everything he knew of Moira.

He said, "I can see now why they wanted a psychic on the crew, Moira. You *knew*, before we were holed. And you knew the damage was in the gym."

"But not in time for it to do us any good," Moira said, tightly. She lowered her eyes and would not look at him.

"I think the first thing for us to do is to deal with the damage in the gym," Teague said, "and to check out all the Life-Support equipment and verify that it's working exactly as it should —"

"No," Peake said steadily. He started shucking his pressure suit. "After this kind of crisis, we're all drained and blood sugar is dropping, so we get panicky and start imagining all kinds of horror. As you said, we're working on stored food, so there's no danger of getting something lethal because the synthesizers aren't working. I suggest we go and have that dinner we were about to have when the meteor struck us."

Only Ravi protested. "I don't want to leave the Bridge until I'm sure we're safely out of proximity to the asteroid belt —"

"At the rate we're going, that will be about six minutes," Peake said shortly, bending to check what he was doing, "and you need food just as much as the rest of us. Anyhow, even if we were out beyond the orbit of Neptune, there would be no way to exclude the possibility of a grain-of-sand type hitting us again. It's about as unlikely as the sun going nova in the next twenty minutes. Come along and have some dinner, Ravi; sitting there in that chair isn't going to keep all the little meteors out of our path!"

"You too, Moira," Ching said, stopping behind her chair. "You'll think more clearly with some food inside you — and I know I will, too."

Peake slung his pressure suit over his arm. He said, "All of you. Bring these, and the helmets, back to the main cabin and store them right where they were. You can see, now, the importance of having them accessible in every module, at every moment!"

As they pushed, one by one, into the free-fall corridor which would take them back to the main cabin where the food console and their musical instruments were stored, Teague bounced up behind Ching. She had taken off the helmet of the pressure suit, and had it tucked under her arm; the heat of the suit made her dark hair cling in wispy little tendrils to the back of her neck. He pried her hands loose from the crawl-bar. "Come on," he said, "I'll hold on to you, I won't let you get hurt. You've got to learn not to be afraid of it, Ching. Come on, put your arms around my neck."

Hesitantly, she complied, feeling his rough cheek against hers. Somehow the feel steadied the lurching sickness inside her. Under ordinary conditions she very much disliked touching anyone, feeling they were all too aware of her difference; she knew how they felt, that she was not quite human. . . as if the genetic tinkering had had some monstrous effect on her, freakishness, and if they touched her, the strangeness would somehow rub off; she had learned to keep herself rigidly away. Only, under the multiple shocks of the past hours, Teague's strength felt warm and comforting, she wanted to cling to him and cry. She wound her arms around him with relief, hiding her face as he pushed off and they flew the length of the corridor, coming up with a soft bump at the far end. Teague pushed her gently through the lock and they were in the familiar gravity of the main cabin. She clambered down from his arms, began to strip off her pressure suit, hanging it in the rack. She felt self-conscious about the way the thin tunic clung, wrinkled and sweaty, to her small breasts.

"I ought to go and shower and put this thing in the disposal!"

Teague chuckled. "We're all the same. Look," he said, laughing at the long rip in the thin nonwoven fiber of his pants, "I'm practically exposed! Not that it makes any difference here, for heaven's sake, we'd all better get accustomed to the sight of each other's bodies. Unless we need clothes for protection, I see no reason we should't go nude at least part of the time. You're not prudish, are you, Ching?"

She shook her head. She had grown accustomed, certainly, to the sight of nude bodies — about half the athletics at the Academy were done co-educationally and in the nude, clothing being worn only where needed for support. Full-breasted women like Fontana had needed some support when running or engaged in active sports. Ching was thin and small-breasted and never needed them; but she had never been one of those who felt more comfortable in the nude, and had in

general worn at least a minimum of clothing. Teague, she remembered, had usually preferred to go naked in the gym or swimming pools. She said, trying not to feel embarrassed at her own unwillingness to do the same, "You don't have to wear clothes for my sake, Teague. Whatever feels comfortable."

"Thanks." Teague stripped off the thin fiber suit and thrust it into a disposal chute. He noticed a stray sheet of the music paper he had covered with a scribbled note, lying on the floor; caught it up and started to send it down the chute after the paper suit, but Ching caught his arm.

"Teague, don't. Finish it first. I really want to see how it comes out, and I'm sure Peake would, too. He's enough of a musician —"

"Enough of a musician not to appreciate anything less than Bach or Mozart," Teague said, wryly, but he did slide the page into the bin which held his flute. Ravi came in, saw Teague's nude body, and said, "That makes sense." He took off his pressure suit, pulling off part of the wrinkled fiber suit under it. As Fontana and Peake and Moira came in through the sphincter, Ravi asked, "Does anyone here seriously object to nudity? We could conserve material for clothing by wearing it only when we're doing dirty work, or want protection."

"I don't mind anyone else going naked," Peake said, "but I like something between my bottom and the seat of the chairs." He hung his pressure suit and helmet in the rack, went and dialed himself some food from the console.

"I handle that by putting a towel or something on the seat," Teague said, taking a small handful of fiber towels from the dispenser at the bottom of the food machine and putting them over the seat. "We recycle the towel material anyhow."

"I don't care who wears what, either," Moira said, "and personally I prefer to go naked about half the time. As long as one thing is made perfectly clear — that it's not a sexual invitation. When it is, I'll make it obvious. If people can distinguish between simple nudity and putting my body up for grabs, I'll go naked. Just don't get the wrong idea, anybody." She stripped off her own crumpled tunic and pants, got herself a plate of food, and sat down to eat.

Ching felt abashed and embarrassed at her own unwillingness to follow suit, as if she were a spoilsport. *I envy Moira's confidence,* she thought. *I wish I could do that.*

Fontana said, "Well, I prefer wearing clothes. My skin is sensitive, and I prefer not to shiver with every stray draft. Anyhow, I prefer to keep nudity for private occasions, if nobody minds."

Ching thought, *well, if Fontana feels that way too, at least I'm not the only one!*

Ravi's eyes followed Moira; her pale skin was freckled all along the back, too, and her small breasts hardly more than brown nipples, the body of a girl of twelve. Fontana and even Ching had more sensuous bodies, but he remembered, with a quick stir of sexual memory, how intensely he desired Moira. Damn; and she had made it very clear how she felt about having that associated with simple nudity. Maybe that was the trouble with nudity, that it was hard to refrain from making those associations here, when you were with a woman you had known. In the gym, or even on the Bridge, where they were deliberately doing something else, he might not have betrayed himself but here he knew he would do so.

Peake watched Teague bringing a tray toward Ching, looking again with appreciation at the heavy layered

muscles, the thatch of curling red hair on Teague's
chest and the matching red patch below. He was acutely
conscious of his own body, thin, dark, gangling, awkward, bones protruding with almost skeletal impact.
Ugly, he thought. *It's not that I'm black. Ravi's darker
than I am and he's beautiful, he's one of the most
beautiful men I've ever seen, but I'm a damned
scarecrow.*

Teague saw the direction of Peake's gaze, and the
interest and admiration in it, and felt suddenly abashed,
turning his eyes away. *Maybe all this nudity wasn't
such a good idea, maybe I shouldn't have started it.*

He carried his own tray over toward Peake and sat
down at the edge of the long seat. He lowered his voice
to where only Peake could hear.

"Listen," he said, with some embarrassment, not
knowing quite how to phrase it, "I can't put it quite the
way Moira did, but does my running around this way
bother you, Peake?"

"Hell, no," Peake retorted good-naturedly, "I was just
admiring the crop of muscles you've got. No matter
how hard I train, and I'm pretty husky and perfectly
fit, I keep on looking like a famine victim!"

"Well, you're an ectomorph," Teague said, feeling
awkward. He moved the tray over his lap, lowering his
eyes, and began to eat, wishing he had not brought up
the subject. Peake said deliberately, "Let's get one thing
straight, Teague. Sure, I like men. I prefer sex with men.
But I don't go around leching about them, not even
when they're running around in the nude; I got used
to that in the gym at the Academy before I was twelve
years old. If I reacted all that much to nude males, I'd
have gone crazy a long time ago. And there's one thing
you'd better realize. I prefer enthusiastic co-operation
in my — shall we say, encounters. Disinterest, or even

tolerance, turns me off — *way* off. And the notion of rape makes me just as sick as it makes any other decent man. Clear?"

Teague stared at his lap and mumbled, "Yeah, clear." And suddenly, perversely, he found himself aware of Peake's slender, dark body, the graceful fingers moving on the spoon. "No offense, Peake?"

"Not a bit," Peake said with deliberate cheerfulness, scooping up the last of this rice, and went to put his plate through the disposal.

Ugly. Ugly as sin. Only Jimson ever thought any different, and he's gone.

Teague went back to Ching, who was picking at the food he had brought her. "You look tense," he said gently. "Here, let me rub your neck." He leaned over her, his firm fingers kneading the tight muscles, feeling her relax, gradually, under his hands. He kept on massaging, transferring the smooth motion down between her thin shoulder blades, and after a bit persuaded her to lie down on the seat, bending over her to knead her back mucles.

She said drowsily, "I'll fall asleep if you keep doing that." She was amazed at herself; once again, her body was betraying her, not this time with sickness, but with a flood of warmth, of lazy, sensuous awareness; she felt that she could lie here forever, with Teague's hands moving on her body.

He leaned over and whispered, his warm breath tickling her ear, "I've got a better idea."

Momentarily Ching went tense under his hands; then, still mesmerized by the caressing movement, she thought, *Why not?* Her body was very alien somehow, she felt she did not recognize it. She let him scoop her up, half-carry her to the door; he held her as they floated through the free-fall corridor.

I cannot trust my body, I cannot trust the computer. But I feel I can trust Teague. Why not? And then, de-fiantly, *Why should I be the only woman in the crew who doesn't know what it is to have sex with a man?*

But in her own cubicle, as he was gently taking off her clothes, a wave of diffidence, of awareness of her own difference, overcame her again.

"Listen, Teague," she said shyly, "I'm not sure I — I mean, I've never done this before, I'm not sure I'll — well, know how. Except, you know, sort of theoreti-cally. Do you mind?"

Teague was overcome with sudden warmth and sym-pathy. He bent close, kissing her, gently prying open her inexperienced lips. He whispered, "No, Ching, I don't mind at all."

CHAPTER TEN

It was Ravi and Moira, in full EVO gear, who approached the building designated the gym through the free-fall corridor, this time slowly, holding to the crawl bar. There was a flaring red light, indicating airlessness and vacuum beyond, and the sphincter had locked automatically, isolating the damaged module. Ravi sealed the first sphincter of the free-fall corridor, so that the corridor could function as an airlock in this emergency, then thrust the tool into the sphincter lock and twisted the lock free. The red light was still blinking.

His pressure-suit audio sounded loud in his own ears.

"Here we go. Let's see what kind of damage we have."

Ravi heard in the audio the sharp breath Moira drew, as the door opened; almost a cry, as if the damage were to her own body. A gaping hole flared in one edge; the meteorite or whatever it had been, had impacted them at tremendous velocity, ripped straight through the module, destroying the rowing-machine Teague had been using as if a bomb had struck it, then, deflected, richocheted and gone out, leaving a surprisingly small hole not really very far from the point of entry.

"Well," he said, trying to make light of it, "looks like we've got a leak in the roof, in here."

Moira giggled; a small, somehow disconsolate sound. Then she noticed that the debris was still lying all over the "floor" of the room, the painted running-track; Ching's ballet barre had been broken by a flying fragment of the rowing machine, holes gouged in the sanded and varnished surface, mats flung about. But the debris lay on the "floor," not strewn, drifting, all over the module.

"There's still gravity in here."

Ravi said, "That's right, the DeMags are still on." He had hoped to find them turned off, damaged by the impact perhaps; then he could have attributed the former DeMag failure to accidental jarring or damage to the control, a hypersensitive control dial.

"Good thing too," Moira said. "Otherwise we'd have to run an obstacle course through floating debris, or tie everything down, before we could start repairing the damage to the module."

"Why couldn't we just have turned it on — oh, that's right; we couldn't trust it not to jolt on hard, the way it did the other day, and everything come raining down hard on top of us," Moira said. "Actually I'm beginning to think the trouble isn't in the DeMags themselves but in the backup system, the fail-safe."

"I'm not sure," Ravi said. "I trust your intuition about machines, certainly. But if that's so, why the failure in the music room the other day?"

"Well, we'll have to check it out," Moira said absently. She was not thinking of Ravi at all, and somehow he felt cold, deserted and lonely. He had known this woman's body, he loved her and cared about her; yet now, facing desolation and destruction and the awareness of barely-escaped death — for if they had all been in the gym, some of them would certainly have been killed — he knew that he was less important to

her than the pieces of Teague's destroyed rowing-machine, which she was dragging together, trying to lay
them out like the broken pieces of a jigsaw puzzle.

*Moira does not love me, not as Jimson and Peake
loved; she does not try to see God in me. I wanted to
see her that way, to feel that the love between us was
a little echo of the Cosmic Love which I am aching to
know. But since the meteor struck, I am nothing to her.*
Ravi set his teeth, grimly accepting this; Moira was not
his property; she had given him sexual access to her,
body, and since she had the right to give it, he knew
that the ethics to which he had been reared demanded
she had also the right to withdraw it, without any reason given, unconditionally. But he hungered for her,
physically, and he felt a deeper desolation which, he
knew, had nothing to do with lust, its frustration or
satisfaction.

"I'd think we might as well put it into the recycler
for molecular conversion," Ravi said. "It's certainly not
worth the trouble of repairing."

She shook her head. "It wouldn't be all that much
trouble; and we don't have the kind of machine tools
we'd need to duplicate it," she said. "I'll have a go at
it, later, when there's time. We'll need the gravity off
in here to go up and repair those holes in the ceiling;
let's secure this for free-fall."

He helped her rope it up, stowing it carefully so that
the broken parts would not drift around in free-fall.
The damage assessed, they went to the storage modules
for patching material, summoned Teague to help them
(Teague being, physically, the heaviest and strongest
of the crew) and turned off the free-fall. Over the next
two ship's days they hammered repairs in place, re-
filled the module with air, tested the seals and sprayed
fiberglass paints over the room, finally sanded and re-

finished the floor. Even the DeMag units tested out perfectly, and when they were finished, Ravi suggested a
celebration.

"What are we celebrating?" Moira asked good-naturedly. "Not that it matters; we don't need an excuse
to throw a party. We could celebrate the passing of the
orbit of Saturn."

"Now that sounds like a good idea," Teague
said, "I'm eager to get some good, close shots of the
rings — "

"We won't be going too close," Ravi told him, "the
rings could be as dangerous as the asteroid belt!"

"I guess what we're celebrating is being well out of
range of the asteroid belt without any more damage,"
Teague said, "or maybe celebrating whatever music we
were playing that kept us out of range of the gym during
that off-time!" During the two days past, they had meticulously stopped work only for the shared music session — all of them had an unspoken agreement that
this was the one daily structure to their lives that would
be violated only in the gravest of emergencies — but
they had slept and eaten and done any other work
aboard the Ship at odd hours.

"Well, officially," Moira said, "what we're celebrating is the re-opening of the gym. I'll be glad to get some
regular exercise at full gravity again." As she spoke she
felt again the twitch of unease, but told herself, sharply,
not to go attributing every little neurotic twitch to her
ESP. She had checked out the DeMags down to the
solid core, this time, and Ching had personally checked
every computer tie-in for the DeMags; it had been the
first thing she had done, since it held the greatest po-
tential for possible dangers.

"We'll make the music session today a party, then,"
Teague said. "I'll speak to Fontana about breaking out

some kind of special meal and drinks, and Ching told me once that she likes to cook, if it's a special occasion and not just routine. I'll ask her about it."

As he spoke of Ching he smiled, and Moira, watching that smile, felt a sudden flare of jealousy. Teague was handsome, strong; she was certain he could give exciting experiences — but she knew Ching was undergoing the first flood of sexual awareness, centered all for the moment upon Teague. She didn't wish to spoil that for Ching. Let her have her first affair untouched by any conflict. She'd learn, soon enough, how little it meant.

Strange, and I admired Ching so much because she didn't feel she had to get involved in this kind of thing, and it turns out she's just like the rest of us. Does everybody do it, then, try to make up for her — or maybe his — own insufficiencies by drowning self-awareness with sex? Look at Ravi, he's still following me around with his tongue hanging out . . . I got so damned tired of that in the Academy, men following me as if I were a bitch in heat, even when I didn't do a thing to turn them on. Sure, sex is fun, but when there's work to do, I like to forget about sex and concentrate on what we're doing! And Ravi's got to learn he doesn't own me.

But as they turned to leave the gym she caught a glimpse of Ravi's unhappy eyes, and a twinge of conscience hit her.

I offered myself to Peake, I said; perhaps it might make you feel less alone. But was I really being kind to Peake, or was I simply intrigued, as he said, by the fact that he was one of the few men I hadn't had? Is that why I want Teague, to satisfy my ego — that I can have any man, even one who's involved with someone else?

*And if I was willing to give myself to Peake to ease
his loneliness, why can't I do the same for Ravi, since
it means so much to him and so little to me?* She wondered why her pride should be so much more important
to her than Ravi's happiness, and then, mentally, she
damned the whole male sex. Really, machinery was
more important, it made no claims, played no elaborate
ego games, and if it was damaged it could be repaired
without any ego involvement. You could handle it as
you wished, and it never made any claims on you, or
complained of how you treated it.

The remainder of the crew welcomed the suggestion
of a celebration; Ching and Fontana readily agreed to
be in charge of a special meal after the music session
that day. Teague asked permission to stay away until
then, claiming that he wanted to photograph the rings
of Saturn from the closest possible approach.

As Ching set the controls for cooking the specially
asked-for foods, she felt strange, conspicuous. Every
control she touched made her acutely aware of the computer tie-ins to Life Support; although she had checked
the hardware inside the computer module, as well as
the control console on the bridge, where it was tied to
Life Support — it had been the first step of a job which
she knew, rationally, was likely to take the better part
of a year, by which time they would be far, far beyond
the Solar System and have reached more than half the
speed of light — she still felt insecure. Her own infal-
libility was shattered beyond repair. Even her body
now felt strange to herself, as if she were no longer in
undisputed possession of it. And Fontana's proximity
made her uncomfortable, too. All her life she had been
aware that camaraderie between women usually came
to an end where rivalry over a man began. It had never
happened to her before because, during her years in

the Academy, she had preserved her withdrawn, sex-
less lack of awareness, and had never challenged any
woman for her male partner. Now, having achieved her
first life-goal, being chosen for crew on the Ship, she
had violated this rule against one of the women she
hoped would be her friend.

One of the first friends she had ever had. She felt
miserable, felt as if she could not face Fontana.

Fontana placed cups — regular disposable plastic,
but somehow she had managed to program them to
come out as cheerful cherry red — around the central
table. "There," she said. "Nothing left but the final
warming, which will take about eighty seconds when
they come in. Shall we pour ourselves a small dividend
to anticipate, Ching, or shall we discipline ourselves
to wait for the others?"

"Let's wait for the others," Ching said, then, suddenly, blurted out, "Are you angry with me, Fontana?"

"Angry with you, Ching? Why? Should I be?"

"Because you and Teague — and now — "

Fontana's first thought was to say an immediate, *My
goodness, no! Don't be silly, Ching!* But a second's
thought changed that impulse; it would seem to take
all too lightly what was all too evidently troubling
Ching. She asked, choosing her words carefully, "Do
you think I have some reason to be angry with you
about that, Ching?"

Ching said, fiddling with the cup and not looking up
at her, "Did you know about — about Teague and —
and me?"

Once again Fontana wondered at Ching's naïveté;
surprising in the self-sufficient, competent Ching. She,
and the other four members of the crew, had all had
a very good idea what was going on, when Teague had
carried Ching out of the main cabin. What else did

Ching think they could have thought? But she only
said, "Yes, I knew. You weren't making any special
effort to hide it, were you?"

"You really don't seem angry," Ching said, surprised,
and Fontana shook her head.

"No, I'm really not angry. Teague isn't my property,
and anyhow — well, Moira said it; it's like one of those
old-fashioned arranged marriages, only there are six of
us. We are going to spend a long, long time together,
all in the same boat and isolated. If any of us starts to
feel as if any other is property, we're in for trouble. I
don't know how much you know about group psychology and social dynamics — I remember you saying
you didn't think of them as very exact sciences,
wouldn't dignify them by the name of sciences or something like that — but it is one of the things people have
found out; that in order to tolerate exclusive or monogamous sexual ties, a group has to be above a certain
crucial number — I think it's eighteen or twenty — so
that the remaining members will have an even chance
at partnerings. We're too small a group to tolerate mo-
nogamy, Ching."

In some obscure way Ching wondered if Fontana
were warning her.

"I'm — well, I'm not used to such things, Fontana.
It was the first time I ever — got myself into a relationship like that. So close."

Fontana, in the calm, rather blank face, saw a sudden
heartbreaking innocence and vulnerability. She said,
very gently, "Do you care about Teague very much,
Ching?"

Ching said, hesitating, "I'm very fond of him. He's —
well, he made it all seem very natural and ordinary, I
always thought I'd be frightened, and I wasn't. I liked
being with him, I enjoyed it. I don't think it was any-

thing like — well, like it was with Peake and Jimson,
I don't think I'm all — all wrapped up in him the way
they were in each other. Only I feel very strange, different inside. Not knowing what to expect of myself
any more, and I've always been so sure. And I don't
think that has anything to do with Teague at all. It has
to do with me."

"Good," Fontana said softly. "You do understand
what I'm saying to you then."

"Only — Fontana, I'm sorry. I mean, because I did
take Teague away from you — if you miss him, I'm
sorry — "

Fontana shrugged and laughed. "That doesn't matter.
Teague is old enough to choose for himself, and so am
I."

"Only — it's what you said. In a group this small
there aren't many choices. It's not as if there were a lot
of men for you to choose from, and you've always had
someone or other, haven't you?"

Ching, Fontana thought, could be so forthright it was
almost alarming. She said, "Well, it's a problem; I suppose it will iron itself out. I don't know what will happen with Ravi and Moira, either. That affair seems to
be rather more off than on, these days. Teague might
decide he wants you for a while, or that he wants me,
or that he wants us both — would that bother you,
Ching?"

She shook her head. She said, "I don't know, I'm not
sure. I don't think so. I told him I wanted to think it
over before — before it happened again. I want to be
sure how I feel. I don't think it's very nice to use a man
to give *myself* confidence."

But even so, Fontana saw her spontaneous bright
smile as Teague came into the main cabin, and almost
envied her. She wasn't jealous about Teague; but she

wished she could recapture that first kind of excitement. *Maybe*, she thought, *it only happens once.*

And I had mine, a long time ago; why envy Ching her own time of discovery? She's waited long enough.

It came back to her, later, when the festive meal was only a few scraps on the plates, and she had begun to collect them and put them into the disposer. After a moment Moira joined her, and said, looking at Teague and Ching, snuggled into one chair, "It looks as if we had the kind of situation aboard that they left Jimson behind to prevent."

"Well, it happens," Fontana said, "and I think Ching has a right to it. But I doubt if it will last long enough to be a threat to the rest of us. Ching's very sensible about it."

"Sensible!" It was a snort, almost a small giggle. "Do you really think that's important?"

"I think she knows what's necessary, for all of us," Fontana said quietly. "For a while I thought it would be you and Ravi."

"Which wouldn't suit you at all, would it," said Moira sharply, "because that wouldn't leave anyone for you except Peake!"

"Why do you assume we have to pair off that way?" Fontana asked.

"No. Seriously, Fontana. What are we going to do about Peake?"

"What makes you think it's up to us to do anything at all about him?" Fontana asked. "He's a grown man, and quite old enough to make his own choices in life. Why do you think we have to do anything?"

"Damn it," Moira shouted so loud that the heads in the room turned to look at them all, "when will you stop answering every question I ask you with another question?"

Fontana said sharply, "When you stop acting as if it was my business to give you answers!"

"You're the psychologist, aren't you?"

Slowly, Fontana shook her head. She said in a low voice, "I'm not anything, Moira, just what the rest of you are. A crew member on the Ship, brainwashed like all the rest of us, to think that making Ship was the end of all our problems. And when I made it, I find out that it's just the beginning of a whole new set of problems! The Academy just threw us out, half-trained, our minds crammed with facts and no real experience. We've already seen that Ching hasn't got all the answers for the computer. Peake's not a doctor, he's a very well-trained medical student. I'm not a psychologist, I've graduated in courses in psychology. You're not an engineer — though you had the experience of assembling the drives in space; you and Teague have had more experience than all the rest of us put together. They throw us out, half trained, to sink or swim, and the odds against any of the Ships surviving are enormous — but just think what's happened to Earth since the first colony was established! They can have their success, it's worth everything to train us and give us these Ships, even if one in ten of us get through — and they can afford not to care about the other nine!"

She stopped herself, forcibly, fighting waves of recurrent horror. *They had been used. All of them! Used, their lives forfeit, since they were five years old. Never told how enormous the odds were against their survival. Yes. The laboratory guinea pig thinks he is petted, pampered, cared for, because he is important in himself. But he is important only to the ones who are using him in their experiment!*

We are all of us just guinea pigs, and probably we are all going to die. And nobody even cares! They put

*a new crop of guinea pigs aboard Survey Ship 103, and
threw us out to live or die!*

*And I can't even throw this out at the others, because
they don't know it yet, they haven't realized . . . . Moira
thinks it's important how our group dynamics work for
survival. Who sleeps with whom. We could all collapse
into anarchy, nihilism, kill one another — we'll die
anyhow!*

"What's the matter, Fontana?" Peake asked, coming
up and taking the stacked armful of disposable plates
from her. "You look awfully tired. Here, let me take
those for you."

She wanted to scream at Peake, *don't be so nice to
me, don't you know we're all going to die, that they
threw us all out to die? We survived the meteor by pure
damn dumb luck . . . . why should I think we'll be one
of the ten who lives instead?*

But before Peake's dark, ugly, kindly face she could
not speak the words. She said, "Thank you, Peake, I —
I guess I am tired."

"Let me get you a glass of wine," Moira said, and
turned to dial the controls. Fontana, controlling herself
by a rigid effort, curled up in a soft chair beside Moira.

"Look," Moira said, "I wasn't trying to intrude on
Peake's private life. But you can't tell me you haven't
thought of it. They sent out three men and three
women, only one of the men is inaccessible, which
means two men for three women, and nobody for Peake.
That doesn't seem to make sense, if they choose the
crews as carefully as they say they do — "

*Haven't you figured it out yet, Moira, that they don't
care, that it's completely random? There are all kinds
of theories about what kind of crew mix will survive,
they can afford to try them all.* For a moment she was
so confused by the words in her mind she wondered

if she had actually spoken them aloud. But Moira was still waiting for her answer. Into the silence Moira said, with unusual shyness, "I — I offered — he turned me down flat. He's all right. For now, anyhow. But it's going to be years, Fontana . . . "

Assuming we live so long. Fontana was growing used to two sets of conversations: what she wanted to say and dared not say, what she really said. Sighing, she said the correct thing.

"Moira, my dear, there is nothing either of us can do about Peake; it's his problem, to face in his own way. Sooner or later, either he will face how he feels about women, and decide to experiment with one of us; or he will persuade one of the men to experiment with him; or he will make a conscious decision to remain celibate and let the rest of us do what we like. And in any case it is his decision. The voyage is only a few days old. We have to give him time. At present it's much more important to you to decide how you feel about Ravi, than to worry about Peake and his problems — or Ching and Teague and *theirs*."

Moira's smile was just a flicker. "I'd swap my problems for Ching's, right now, but I don't know if she'd care to trade. I'm glad she's enjoying herself, anyhow. I wish I were."

CHAPTER ELEVEN

Ching startled awake with a cry, the sharp nightmare
shock, the old atavistic terror of *falling* . . . no, she was
not falling, the sleeping net held her closely restrained;
but it was the floor that was not anywhere, she was
floating, spinning, no down or up, no orientation —
she felt her stomach heave, heard herself moan, and
shut her eyes against the impact of it, struggling with
sickness.

This was absurd; of course there was only one explanation, the damned DeMag units were off again in
her cubicle. Was it through the whole of the living
quarters? Or only in her own cubicle, or what? She
clung to the bunk, frozen, incapable of what she knew
she ought to do; clamber down and turn the DeMag
unit firmly off, then on again, to bring back the needed
gravity. She fought to force her fingers to unclip the
sleeping net, let herself slide along the bunk, clinging
to the rails as to a crawl bar. Yet her inner-ear channels
convinced her that the bunk, which ought to be in an
orderly spot halfway between floor and ceiling, was
somehow suspending her upside-down at a crazy, sickening angle.

She shouted, "Hey!" Had this happened in all the
cubicles? Had anyone else been awakened by it? Would

anyone else even notice, far less be awakened by that
nightmare plunge? They all seemed to manage, somehow, none of the others felt that sickening physical
disorientation and terror. In response to her cry there
were a few sleepy sounds, and then Teague thrust his
sinewy shoulders through the opening of the cubicle,
and made strong swimming motions up toward the
bunk where she clung. He unclipped the safety net and,
clasping her tight in his arms, propelled them both
down to the floor.

"Poor love, poor little thing," he murmured, stroking
her hair, "were you frightened? You should have called
out before, only I thought it was only in my own cubicle; I should have come in and checked to make sure
you were all right."

She hid her face against Teague's naked chest, wondering why she felt so boneless, so wholly devoid of
strength in his arms. Could a simple biological process,
even when aided by hormones, do that to her, or was
it simply a matter of suggestion and psychology, was
it all in her mind after all?

Still holding her in the circle of one arm, he slid
down toward the DeMag unit, turned the dial firmly off
and then on again. Ching, still holding her breath and
struggling against nausea, felt the world blessedly settle
down to normal again.

"Are you all right, sweet? I'd better check up on the
others, and then I'll be right back," Teague promised.
She heard his voice, calling out to the rest of them, one
after the other, reassuring them.

"I guess it was only your cubicle, and mine, Ching,
everyone else seemed to be all right."

"Did — it — wake you?"

He shook his head. "No, I was awake, working. Working on my string quartet; it's not going the way I want

it to go. I really don't have the training in theory that
I need. And I'm not a good enough violinist to know
whether the things I write are playable or not. Theoretically, they *should* be, but I can't really imagine if
they would sound the way I expect them to sound. And
I don't know how to resolve it."

"Ask Peake to play them for you," Ching suggested.
Teague had crawled into the bunk beside her, clipped
the safety net over them both; he lay on his side, facing
her, his face almost invisible in the dimness; there was
no light except the dim rim of illumination just outside
the door of the cubicle, but as her eyes grew accustomed
to the dark she could make out that he looked dejected.

"Peake? No, I couldn't. He's a real musician. He's
used to great music, or at least to the computer doing
things *right*, and my stuff is so crude. I'd be ashamed
to show it to Peake."

"Don't be foolish, Teague. He likes you, he'd be glad
to tell you what's good about it and what's wrong with
it — "

"That's what I'm afraid of," Teague muttered.

"Even if it was awful, Teague — and honestly, I don't
think it is — Peake is much too nice to be rude to you
about it, or make fun or you. He'd understand what
you were trying to do, and I'm sure he'd be nice and
helpful."

"That's not what I'm worrying about," Teague said,
his face buried in her neck, so that she could hardly
hear the words. "I wouldn't mind how rude he was, or
how much he made fun of it, if he levelled with me.
What I'm afraid of is that he'd just be — be *nice* about
it. Nice and polite, and not take it seriously. How could
anybody take it seriously, writing string quartets in this
day and age? It's like writing sonnets. Peake would
think it was sort of quaint and cute and be ever so nice

about it. Kind and, well, condescending, but he wouldn't
take it seriously as music, he *couldn't*."

"How can you possibly know that without asking
him?"

"Oh, well, maybe I will," said Teague, in such an
offhanded way that Ching knew he wouldn't. "Are you
all right now, not feeling sick any more?"

"Oh, yes. Thank you, Teague, you don't have to stay
with me any more . . . "

"But I want to," he whispered holding her close.
"You don't mind, do you? Let me stay, Ching."

She knew that she should make him go, she had
resolved that she would make him go, it was not right
to use Teague this way, to give herself confidence, to
hold her fears and loneliness at bay.

We are all foolish, she thought. *Teague is foolish
about showing his music to Peake. And I am foolish
too, I let Teague stay when I should make him go, learn
to cope with these fears on my own!*

"Have you tried making in love free-fall?" Teague
urged. "It's fun, it's like flying . . . "

Much as she wanted to please him, Ching flinched
from the idea. She said ruefully, "I don't think you'd
have much fun with me vomiting all over you."

"Oh, you're doing better, you didn't get sick this
time — "

"I almost did, though. If it had lasted any longer, I
would have," Ching said, and Teague hugged her.
"Well, we'll work on it. But it's a good thing, sometimes, free-fall. For instance, my weight wouldn't be
so heavy on you — you're so tiny, I'm always afraid I'll
crush you beneath me!"

"I don't mind," she murmured, drawing him down
to her, and for a time they did not talk at all, only
murmuring, soft love-sounds.

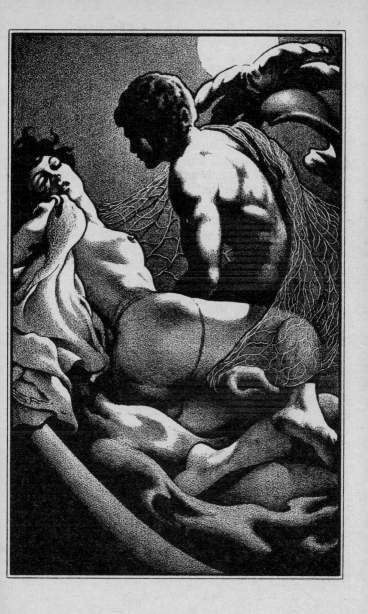

A considerable time later, she asked him, "Where did you have experience making love in free-fall? Was it in Lunar Dome?"

"No, it was here on the Ship," Teague said. Her eyes were dilated enough to the dark now that she could see his face clearly. "Fontana — you don't mind my talking about that, do you, Ching?"

"No, no, of course not," she said, "Fontana and I were talking about that. I know there aren't enough of us for — for any kind of permanent pairings. And, Teague, you don't have to choose between us, really. I don't mind, if you want Fontana sometimes —"

"I know that," he said gently, petting her, "but I'm glad you can be sensible about it, too, Ching. It's going to be a long trip. Even provided we get the computer fixed."

"We will," she said, "I've gone through a lot of the connections, and found out where some of the trouble might be. I can't imagine what they were thinking of in Lunar Dome when they assembled it; I wish I'd been there when it was done, it would have made my work so much easier now. At least you had a chance to help install the drives!"

"Along with Fly and Dolly and Duffy and Perk," he said, smiling, "and each of us wondering if it would be our one and only sight of the Ship."

"Are you glad you were chosen, Teague? Really?"

"I'm not sure," he said, at last, slowly. "It happens, it's done, there's no chance for second thoughts. I spent my life wanting to be Ship when our class graduated. Now, I wonder. Maybe that's just let down. But yes, I suppose I'm glad. It's an adventure. It's real."

She yawned, tucking her hands behind her head. She said, "I think we ought to try and get some more sleep; I have work to do. I would think making love in free-fall would be a lot of trouble. Every time you moved, you and — the other person — would go flying apart . . . "

"Oh, you do, unless you're careful," Teague said. "You have to do it with a safety net clipped on, or one of you could crack your head against the wall and get a concussion. But it's fun. Free-fall is fun, Ching, only you have to learn to relax, to go with the flow, be willing not to be in control all the time. Just let it happen. Just surrender to it."

Although he had spoken gently and without any personal emphasis, Ching felt her cheeks flushing with heat, aware that she had still the horror of losing control, surrendering — whether in free-fall or in sex. She said, trembling, "I don't *want* to be afraid of free-fall. Teach me to like it, Teague, the way you do."

"I will," he promised, "Later today. But sleep now, Ching. We have a lot to do — and everything should be verified and the final course corrections made before we leave the Solar System."

"We still have three days," Ching murmured. "Anything could happen in that time."

Curled against Teague, she slept.

"Did you find anything in the DeMag tie-ins?" Moira asked.

Ching stretched, wriggling free of the computer module. "So far, nothing. There is absolutely no reason why the DeMag units should go on and off like that, and therefore, going by pure logic, they should stay on unless they are turned off, and stay off unless they are turned on."

"But the fact is that they don't," Moira said, "and it doesn't make sense! Dammit, Ching, I like machinery to make sense, to do what it's designed to do. When it starts acting temperamental, it's no better than a man!"

"Are all men really that bad, Moira?" Ching murmured.

"All of them. No exceptions. Believe me."

"Well," Ching said, with a wisp of a smile, "you should know."

Moira flung back her head and laughed. "I think you'll do, Ching. I was beginning to think you were just too sweet and kind to be true, but that remark sounded quite normally catty!"

Ching raised her straight brows, ironically. "Thank you, my dear. Coming from you, I'm sure that's intended for a compliment!"

They laughed together. Ching found herself wondering why, suddenly, Moira treated her as one of them. Was it, simply, that she had felt different, before this — and that Moira had been reacting to her, Ching's, perceived difference, instead of any real difference? Did the fact that she was a G-N really make as much difference as she had always believed? If she had felt more like one of them, would they have treated her that way?

Had her isolation been, somehow, of her own making?

"I promised to meet Teague in the gym," Ching said, moving past her, and Moira, suddenly frightened, caught at her arm to detain her. But what was she going to say? It was not as clear as a psychic warning, just a faint, strange unease. She tried to make a joke of it.

"You should always keep a man waiting, just a little. Never let them be sure of you."

Ching laughed gently. "Is that the way you treat Ravi? I'd rather make Teague happy than unhappy, Moira."

"Yes, I suppose you would," said Moira, with a strange bitterness. But again she touched Ching's arm, as if to hold her back.

"Ching — be careful."

"I will," Ching promised, startled, and, seeing the troubled look in Moira's green eyes, sensed that the other girl was distressed; though she didn't know why. She hugged Moira, gently, and kissed her cheek. She had never felt close enough to either of the other women to do this before.

"I will, Moira. Don't worry," she promised, and went. Moira stood looking after her for a little while, frowning, wishing she could identify the angry unease she felt. *That damned gym,* she thought with sudden violence, *I wish the meteor had carried it right away off the Ship! Is any of us ever going to feel safe there again? Here I am dithering for no reason!*

Ravi found her in the main cabin, idly leafing through some music.

"Are you going to the Bridge?"

"In a minute," she said absently. "It's time to make the routine sail-trim." She drew a deep breath. She enjoyed manipulating the sails to optimum light-pressure; since the meteor damage and the varying DeMag failures, and the terrifying failure of the computer, she felt a definite pleasure in something like the sails, which did exactly what she wanted them to do, exactly as she wanted them.

When I was in primary division they called me manipulative. I suppose, when you come right down to it, I am.

"The sails can wait a minute," said Ravi firmly. "I have to talk to you, Moira. Why are you avoiding me?"

"Don't be silly, my dear," Moira laughed, "I see you all the time, just as I do all the rest of us."

"You know what I mean." He took her hand lightly in his; she started to pull it away, then sighed and let

it lie in his; but so limp and passive that he knew she
was simply avoiding an argument. Pulling her hand
away would have been less offensive.

"Why have you changed, Moira?" he asked, "We
were happy for a few days, and then — then you turned
me right off. Don't you care at all about me?"

She said, irritably, "Oh, Ravi, don't. I'm your friend,
and we agreed to keep it that way. I'm not ready for
any kind of emotional, romantic relationship — I don't
think I ever will be. Most people believe as I do, that
romance is a kind of mental aberration. We've got sex
and we've got friendship, and if that's not enough for
you — well, I'm sorry, but I won't be pressured into
something I don't want. If you're horny, go and sleep
with Fontana — now that Teague's all wrapped up in
Ching, she's probably lonely and hard up for a man in
her bed."

Ravi said quietly, "How can you be so cynical, Moira?
Don't you even know how much I care about you?"

"I know," she said languidly, "and nothing has ever
bored me so much in my life."

Ravi recoiled as if she had struck him. But he resolved to make one further effort. Surely, if she understood, she would be less unkind.

"Moira, I don't know how to say this. Ever since —
since before we left Earth, I've been looking — looking
for something. Please don't think I am foolish — it's a
kind of," he hesitated, "a spiritual search, a longing for
something greater than humanity, and I, I think I've
found it. It's what Peake and Jimson were groping toward, trying to find a kind of completion in each other.
A fulfilment. I, I, I — " he was stammering in his ur-
gency to communicate something of what he felt, "I'm
trying to find the Cosmic, the universe, God if you like,
and I am trying to find it, to worship God in you,

Moira — do you see what I'm trying to say?"

Moira stared at him, appalled, bored, angry, half tempted to puncture him with a flippant obscenity. Instead she said, in a flat hard voice, "I can only imagine that you are going insane, Ravi. Maybe you've been staring out the window too much. You'd better keep your eyes on the Navigation instruments, or it won't take a computer failure to send us to nowhere. I never heard such rubbish in my life."

Ravi drew a sharp, shaking breath, wounded, and for a moment she hoped he would fling something insulting at her, give her a chance to justify her words. Instead he kept on looking at her, and finally said, almost inaudibly, "I suppose I can't expect you to feel any other way. But I love you, Moira. Try and remember that."

He stood up and went out of the cabin.

In the gym, Teague knelt and set the gravity to one-half of normal. "Does this bother you?" he asked.

"N-no," Ching said, "As long as there's enough to know whether I'm right-side-up or upside-down." Was that what he had meant by fighting to stay in control?

"Here, try the springboard," he said "Spring up in the air and somersault; and let me catch you in midair. I won't let you fall, I promise you."

Hesitantly, Ching sprang up from the board, letting her narrow body spin free in a double somersault in midair; felt Teague's arms clasp around her and they spun the length of the gym in a single soaring leap.

After a few more maneuvers, feeling that Ching seemed somehow less frightened, Teague went back to the controls.

"All the way off, this time?"

She looked at him, scared and yet exhilarated, given confidence by his own ease in midair. Then she nod-

ded, laughing a little, breathless. "I don't think I could
be afraid of anything when you were with me, Teague."

With a decisive movement, Teague turned the controls all the way to OFF, felt himself float upward and
made a bound to catch Ching as she drifted free. She
laughed again, clasping him in her arms, letting him
soar with her the full length of the gym, giving herself
over to the strange, empty, falling sensation.

"You're right, Teague, it is fun when you don't try
to fight it!" She slid from his arms, soaring free, spinning dizzily around the room, her laughter still high
and breathless as she leaped toward the ceiling, flew
downward. He bounded after her as she took off like
a swallow, arms folded, soaring.

Teague felt the sudden, hard jolt, put out a hand to
save himself; came down on one wrist, feeling agony
tearing through the tendons as the wrist let go; clasped
it, with a cry of pain, fighting to recover his balance;
the movement ripped lightnings of renewed pain
through his arm as he ran, but too late. Ching fell like
a stone, striking head-first, and lay still.

Peake was on the Bridge with a silent, sullen Ravi,
doing the painstaking work of triangulation from four
points of reference to work out the Ship's precise position; a necessary, daily ordeal until they could absolutely trust the computers again.

"I hope Ching gets that finished before we leave the
Solar System," Ravi muttered.

"There's no way she could do that. Not if she worked
round the clock," Peake said, "and she's been virtually
doing that; she stops for meals and a two-hour exercise
period and the daily music session, and the rest of the
time she's been wedged inside the computer module,
where for all I know she's tearing the infernal thing to
pieces! She estimated another ten days when I asked

her, and that's assuming she can keep up that murderous routine without her health or morale suffering."

"She's not in the computer now, is she?"

Peake shook his head. "I think she's probably sleeping; she and Fontana were sorting some music, some fairly archaic duets they wanted to try singing. Or she and Teague may have gone off to their cabins for a bit of rest and recreation — so to speak. And they're certainly entitled, the way they've been working to repair everything."

"I wish I could do something to help," Ravi said, "but inside the computer I'd be about as much help as a snowball inside a nuclear reactor."

Peake looked at the small, dark man with sympathy. He said, "I know, I hate feeling helpless. I do feel they should have sent a second computer technician; if I had been making the decisions, I'd probably never send a crew smaller than ten. It would make the trip easier on all of us, too. But as things are, we simply have to do what we can in our own fields, and let the others do theirs. At that, I suspect that if Ching picks someone to teach, in order to have a backup computer technician, you'll probably be the one. You're a natural mathematician — and on top of that, you're physically small enough to fit into the computer module. I understand that makes a difference."

"So Ching said," Ravi agreed, "and I admit I'd be interested. There was a time, when we started choosing specialties, that I considered computer work. But having started with navigation and astronomy, I felt that meteorology and oceanography would be more useful; two specialities for in space, two for any planet we were surveying."

"That's what they usually recommend," Peake said. "I wish there had been a Navigation first specialist, though. When I think of all the trouble they would have saved if they had added another four people to the crew. Another navigator. Another computer tech. At least. Maybe another medic. Perhaps another engineer."

"I don't understand why they didn't," Ravi said, "and of course we'll never know. I'd have been glad to have Mei Mei, or Fly, or even Jimson . . . "

"It wouldn't have bothered you, Ravi? To have both of us?"

Ravi shook his head. He said, "No, certainly not. I liked Jimson, though he was a little — well, unpredictable. No more so, certainly, than Moira, though." And pain moved suddenly in him again. He did not believe that what he felt for Moira was a neurotic obsession. He simply wanted to love her, cherish her, treat her as the other half of himself, to love her as his own soul, the female part of his humanity. She had so completely misunderstood him. He did not want to possess her; if she desired other men she was free to have them, he did not want in any way to narrow her horizons, but only to help her expand them to cosmic limits. And she had rejected this, rejected it entirely. He loved her no less for the rejection; it still seemed to him that in loving Moira he had learned more about love, about the secrets of awareness locked at the heart of life; only now it seemed to him that instead of God's self being centered somewhere in the great, eternal, infinite vastness of stars out there beyond the window of the Bridge, he was somehow linked to that cosmic pulsing, and that its echo was here within the focus of the Ship, that it was in his comrades here. It was within Moira, within himself, within all of the others, and even Peake's craggy face seemed infinitely beautiful to him, infinitely worthy of love and even worship. He

knew that if he carried this even a little further it would
dissolve into sentiment and self-pity, but now he
looked at Peake and felt, with an overflow of pure and
unsentimental emotion, that he would give his life for
him, or for any of them, and that he would not even
notice the difference. As long as one of them lived he
would continue to survive as part of the cosmic unity
he felt flowing among them all. Even the pain and regret
he felt because Moira had refused his love was irrelevant; he had somehow moved to a point where pain
and pleasure were irrelevant and interchangeable. He
would love Moira, he would continue to pour out his
love upon her, as upon God, uncaring whether she accepted it, or even knew about it; his mistake had been
in telling her about it, the love was no less because she
did not return it. Describing the position of the Ship
among the stars, entering it formally in the log, he felt
somehow that he had described his relationship to God
with the numbers.

This new state of mind was so unexpected, so much
a strangeness, that he actually stopped a moment to
wonder, *Am I going insane, is this exultation only in-
sanity's dangerous leading edge of euphoria? Maybe
I should talk to Fontana about it.* And yet he was functioning perfectly well, his mathematical calculations
were impeccable — for Peake, duplicating his work on
the calculator, had validated them to the last decimal
place — he was making accurate observations, his body
performed exactly as well as he told it to, he was eating
normally, digesting his food, and playing music with
the others, not going off on some ecstatic trip of his
own. His pulse, respiration, color perception, blood
pressure, and urine were all normal, or so Peake had
pronounced them at the regular three-day medical
checkups. He reacted well to normal gravity, to partial

gravity and to free-fall. Therefore he assumed he was physically and mentally normal, in an abnormal emotional state.

Maybe abnormality is in the mind of the Beholder?

Even the feeling that I partake of God does not give me any delusions of omnipotence. I personally am a very small and helpless part; but I perceive myself as a very real part, partaking in the Whole. I do not feel dwarfed by the immensity of Space, but enlarged; I am part of the Whole, and the Whole is part of me.

And this religious consciousness does not make me less sane, but saner, if functioning is any criterion of sanity.

He even felt hungry, and said so.

"It's dinner time fairly soon," Peake said, yawning, 'Twenty minutes standard, more or less. Teague said he was going to begin synthesizing carbohydrate, fairly soon. I'll probably miss having normal rice and wheat grains, won't you?"

"I doubt if I'll be able to tell the difference," Ravi admitted. "Where I'm concerned, a carbohydrate is a carbohydrate, and the shape doesn't matter. I never could understand the tribes who starved to death rather than eat wheat when rice was their preferred staple, or eat rice when wheat was scarce or unavailable."

Peake's smile was wry. "Maybe that's why we survived instead of dying, man. I survived one famine year when I was about five, and as I remember, I ate anything I could cram into my mouth without worrying what it was. I still get the nightmare about that, sometimes. Hungry, and no food anywhere. Then I remember being tested for the Academy, and at first all it meant to me was, never hungry no more. That's what my uncle said to me when he took me there . . . hey, look, we're not supposed to talk about the past, are we?"

"I don't think it does any of us any harm," Ravi said gently. "Come on, Peake, we're finished here. Let's go down to the main cabin . . . "

He broke off, for the intercom had leaped into sudden life.

"Peake, Peake," it said, "Peake, Peake, anybody, anybody down here — Peake, Fontana, somebody, come quick, there's been an accident, oh, come help, somebody — "

"Teague!" It was like an expletive; Peake was out of his seat within seconds. Ravi said urgently into the intercom, "Teague, where are you? Are you hurt?"

"In the gym. Damn DeMags . . . "

Peake cut him off. "I'm on my way. Ravi, go back to the main cabin and get my medical kit — I'll go straight there, I could save some time — "

But in the entry to the free-fall corridor outside the gym he bumped into Fontana, and she had his medical bag in her hand. "I heard Teague on the intercom and I knew you'd need this," she said. "Hurry, Peake!"

He pushed through the sphincter lock ahead of her; took in Teague, kneeling over Ching; noted the limp dangle of one hand, dismissed it to fumble quickly for a pulse in Ching's limp wrist. Yes, it was there, feeble but definite. There was a small blue bruise on her temple, bloodless.

"Fontana," Peake said tersely, "you fix up Teague's wrist, or hand, while I find out what's wrong with Ching. Teague, tell me what happened? Did the gravity go off?" In his mind was a clear memory of the time when he had nearly crashed into a wall while running; luck and superb co-ordination had saved him at least a concussion, perhaps a skull fracture. Ching had not been so lucky.

"The gravity *was off*," Teague said. "It went on." He

was sobbing, covering his face with his good hand. "She wanted to learn to handle herself in free-fall, I talked her into it, oh, God, it's my fault — I promised I wouldn't let her fall, I promised I wouldn't let her get hurt, she trusted me, oh, she trusted me and I let her fall — "

He was clearly hysterical; Fontana snapped, "Shut up and let me get this wrist bandaged! You can't do any good by blubbering!" She chose the word deliberately, and it shut him up with a gasp.

"Now try and tell us coherently," she said, "exactly what happened."

Teague took a deep breath; cried out in sharp pain as Fontana manipulated his wrist.

"Broken finger here," she said to Peake, "fourth finger, left hand. Probably need a splint. Possible damaged tendons or ligaments. Those damned, infernal De-Mags!" She set her mouth tightly, and continued manipulating Teague's hand. "Wriggle that finger. Here, does that hurt? Good, that's all right. What did you do, come down hard on it?"

"Ravi," Peake said, "try and find ammonia in the bag. Small vial, glass ampoule — yes, that's it." He broke it under Ching's nose, wondering if the glass fragments would scatter and be dangerous in the case of another DeMag failure. He wanted to get her out of there, but he didn't dare to move her until he was certain there were no spinal injuries; and he couldn't tell that until she was conscious.

Ching stirred fractionally and opened her eyes.

"Teague — " she whispered.

"I'm here, darling. Don't move."

"What happened? Teague, move out of the way, please — " Peake said, bothered by the intrusion, but watching Ching's hands groping for him, he was re-

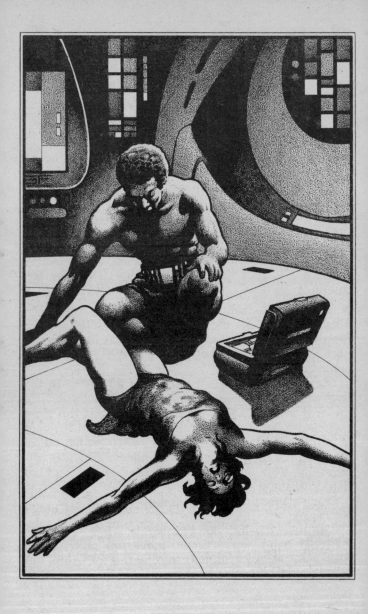

lieved. No gross damage to the spinal cord, at least, if she could move her hands. He slipped off the thin fiber sandals she was wearing.

"Ching, can you wriggle your toes?" But she had shut her eyes again and drifted off into unconsciousness.

He had to know. Quickly he selected a probe from the bag, ran it quickly along the sole of her foot, was rewarded by a strong flinching and twitching of the toes. He felt immensely relieved; no paralysis. Concussion, certainly, and in view of her stuporous state, they could not even rule out a skull fracture; but there was no spinal cord damage and, at least, it was safe to move her. Not that there was any absolute safety anywhere. There had been DeMag failures in the main cabin and in the living quarters, which meant that the trouble with the DeMags was not confined to the unit in the gym; it had to be in the computer tie-ins, or else some major design flaw in the units themselves, or the controls on the units.

In shock, Peake remembered: Ching was their only access to the computer! Damn the people at the Academy who had let them go out with only a single computer technician! Remembering his conversation with Ravi, he damned them further.

If Ching was badly hurt, or worse — he flinched away from remembering that head injuries were the most commonly fatal of all injuries — the computer might never be wholly trustworthy again.

In which case, they were probably all doomed . . . .

Rising to his full height, he angrily brushed that thought aside. It was more than probable that Ching's injury was only a minor concussion; most head injuries, after all, were no more. He said, "We've got to rig a stretcher. There's no way we can get her through that free-fall corridor without one."

"It's not going to be any too easy even with one,"
Fontana said. "Ravi, you're able-bodied, go and find
Moira and get her to help you rig something to carry
Ching; she's about the best mechanic aboard."

Even with Ching's unconscious body firmly strapped
to a stretcher and a safety net stretched over her to
immobilize her, it was not at all easy; Peake, weighing
danger against danger — in head injuries any kind of
depressant was dangerous — finally took out a pres-
sure-spray hypo and gave her a shot. He explained
tersely, to Fontana's raised eyebrows — she had had a
secondary specialization in medicine, enough to make
her a competent technician or assistant — "If she vom-
its in free-fall while she's unconscious, she could as-
pirate vomit, and you know as well as I do what that
would do to her lungs. It would be safer not to move
her at all. But I don't trust the DeMags in here even as
much as I trust the ones in the main cabin."

But Ching did not stir or show the slightest sign of
distress as the stretcher, guided by Peake at one end
and Fontana at the other, was floated carefully down
the corridor and maneuvered through the sphincter
locks. They swept music hastily to one side and laid
her on the table in the main cabin.

Paradoxically, though he did not wish Ching any
distress and was glad she was spared the ordeal of
vomiting in free-fall, her very failure to do so troubled
Peake. Interfering with that reflex action, necessary as
it was, would make it even harder to diagnose accu-
rately what, if any, damage she had sustained; nausea
was a good and accurate gauge of the depth of concussion. Grimly he recalled a hospital tenet from his training; better complaining than comatose! The more
miserably sick Ching had been, the better he would
have felt about her.

He folded back an eyelid to check the pupils of her eyes; flashed a light, and set his teeth, knowing there was trouble. The two pupils were unequally dilated; and ammonia failed, this time, to rouse her to consciousness. He got out a set of probes and started pricking her feet with them.

"You're hurting her," Teague protested, as he slid the probe under a toenail; Teague could feel his own toes shrink in sympathy, but Peake looked alien, grim, distant. "I wish I *could* hurt her," he said. "Damn it, Teague, I'm not being brutal, I have to check how much she's responding to painful stimuli!"

"Oh. Right." Teague shut up, looking miserably at the stranger Peake had suddenly become; distant, frighteningly efficient, not at all the good-natured, soft-spoken crew member, but vested with all the charisma, power and authority of Medicine. Ching too had become wholly strange, limp and apparently lifeless, her face without expression as if cast in marble, the bland meaningless features in cold and chiselled silence. Her small blue-veined foot was like a baby's foot, the sole soft and pink as if it had never been walked on. There was a small spot of blood where Peake had driven the probe under the nail.

And less than an hour ago she had been laughing in his arms; the memory of her words tore at him with agony and guilt.

I don't think I could ever be afraid of anything, with you, Teague!

And I could let this happen to her! He put his hands over his face again and began to weep softly, trying not to disturb Peake, who was, with grim concentration, testing responses. Once or twice he made a small sound of approval; but mostly his craggy black features grew grimmer and more set.

Finally he covered Ching with a blanket, and straightened, sighing. He flinched, seeing four faces turn to him as if — the thought came to him without volition — they were waiting for the word of God.

How am I to do that? For the first time since he had begun his serious hospital training — at the age of fourteen — he realized how desperately unprepared he was for this kind of thing. He had surgical and medical experience, certainly; the kind that would be presumably needed among healthy young people. He could splint a fracture, repair a serious compound fracture or severe muscular injury, deal with the most common accidents and traumas; he had taken out a round dozen of appendixes and gall bladders, sewed up any number of wounds, even assisted at several deliveries and done the odd Caesarean section. But complex neurological problems — and it looked as if this was turning into a major one — were beyond him. He had the book knowledge but no experience with them.

I might as well not be a doctor at all, just a glorified medical student!

They were still waiting, every face depending on his word. He drew a deep breath, trying to sound more confident than he felt.

"It's not good," he said, "but it may not be all that serious. Everything is going to depend on keeping her quiet and undisturbed and on what happens in the next two or three hours. It may be simple concussion, in which case she will get well without any further trouble, except for needing rest and quiet. If it's more serious — a depressed skull fracture, or if there's bleeding somewhere inside the skull — well, then it could be very, very serious. But there's no point in worrying about that until we're sure. We don't have X-Ray equipment; they didn't foresee any such serious medical emergencies. If we did, we could rule out a fracture, one way or the other, right away. But we don't. So we have to wait and see; if she gets worse, that will mean it's serious, and if she doesn't, that will mean that it isn't." He bared his teeth in a nervous grimace. "For all our medical technology, that's the ultimate primitive medicine — wait and see."

"But we can't sit here and do *nothing*," Moira burst out in shock. "Suppose she — she just dies while we're waiting?"

That was simple hysteria and Peake took refuge in textbook answers; not answering the question but the anxiety behind it.

"Moira, she could have been picked up dead from the floor in there; we are better off than we would have been in that case, because she *is* still alive. Anything I do now, without knowing precisely what the problem is, could only make it worse."

As he had known it would, his air of total control and confidence silenced them for the moment. The Doctor had Spoken, and for the moment, at least, all was well. *If only they knew how little I feel like a Medical Authority at this moment! It's probably just as well they don't.*

"Now," he said, "we should leave Ching in quiet. Get some food out of the console — anything you can get quickly and quietly — and leave the main cabin to her. Go to your living quarters, or to the Bridge, or wherever you wish, but this place has to be kept quiet, preferably kept dark. I'll stay here and monitor her vital signs every few minutes. As long as she's still responding, there's nothing to worry about. If she should stop responding, then there's — well, we'll cross that bridge when we come to it."

One by one, sobered, they went to the food console,

dialed themselves some quick and easy rations, and started to carry them out of the room.

Teague said, "Can't I stay with her, Peake? I'll be quiet, I won't disturb her, I promise."

Peake shook his head. "It wouldn't do either of you any good. At this moment, even if she should come around and ask for you, the last thing she needs is your guilt! It's absolutely imperative that if she wakes up, she should be kept quiet, should just lie there and vegetate, without being disturbd in any way. And if she doesn't — well, that would be harder on you. 'I'll send for you the minute you can do anything helpful, believe me, Teague."

But while the others were collecting trays of food, more, Peake suspected, from habit than hunger, he approached Fontana.

"You're the only other one with any medical training," he said, very low. "If Ching doesn't come around within a few hours, you know what it will mean: either a subdural or a depressed fracture. Either way, you know what that will mean." He stared down at his hands, steadying them by an act of will. He said, more to himself than to Fontana, "It's a simple operation, really. The Egyptians did it with their flint knives,and people lived through it; there's evidence of new bone growth to prove that they lived years afterward."

But inwardly, beneath the calmness, he was thinking; *my first really major surgery, and it has to be on the brain. And on a friend!*

Was this why they separated me from Jimson? If he had been the one hurt, could I have operated on him? Were they deliberately isolating me, so that as a surgeon I could be detached?

He kept his voice calm. "If I do have to operate, you'll have to assist, you're the only one who could manage it. You'd better be prepared for it; I hope it won't come to that. But we may have to do it, as a last resort."

And then he was frightened; for Fontana stared at him, her eyes wide, blank, expressionless, as if she were in shock. Her mouth twitched.

And then she said, harshly, her voice like a shriek, "Damn you, Peake, how stupid you are! Haven't you figured it out yet? Do you really think there's anything we can do? You know as well as I do that this whole Crew business is a final test, and we're just the ones who failed, that's all! Not the ones who passed triumphantly, just the ones they thought they could spare! The Academy throws us out, every year, like spores, Ship crews going out to sink or swim, live or die, probably ninety out of a hundred of the Ships have died already, but it doesn't matter, as long as one or two Ships get through to establish us on the stars — that's all they care about, as long as one in a hundred might get through! We don't have proper equipment, not even an X-ray — doesn't that show you how little they care about our survival? Look at her!" She gestured at Ching's blanketed, silent form. "She's the only one of us who knows anything about computers, and we have a major computer failure — if they really cared about whether we survived, wouldn't they create more of a backup system? We don't even have any way to communicate with Earth in an emergency! Peake, we're dead, don't you see? Even if she lives, she could be a vegetable, massive brain damage, never be able to fix the computer — if she dies, she's just the lucky one who died first! And you're thinking about saving her life with a major brain operation — you, a half-trained medical student they crammed with a few facts and sent off thinking you were a surgeon? Forget it, Peake! We're going to die, that's all there is to it, and we've

just got to accept it!'' Her voice rose to a scream. ''Accept it! Accept it! We're dead, dead, dead, we're all of
us dead! This whole Crew business is just a sick, horrible joke! We're the salmon swimming upstream, the
lemmings plunging out into space — and we're one of
the ones who didn't make it, we're dead, all of us,
dead!''

Shocked silence in the main cabin. Peake blinked,
squeezing his eyes shut at the vehemence of her rage.
*Fontana! Fontana, of all people, the calm one, the psy-
chologist, the one who helped everyone else with their
problems — if she could blow loose this way, was there
even a grain of hope for any of them?*

Fontana thought not . . . .

But Peake acted without thought, from his training;
by sheer reflex. He swung back his hand and slapped
Fontana hard, right across the mouth.

''Shut up,'' he said, his voice cold and clipped, ''I
will not have my patient disturbed with this kind of
hysterical nonsense.''

''It's not hysteria and it's not nonsense and you know
it,'' Fontana screamed at him.

Peake gestured with a quick movement of his head.

''Moira. Teague. Get her out of here. Take her to her
quarters, give her a shot of tranquilizer if you have to —
Teague, you're on Life Support, you know the stuff.
Knock her out, sit on her if you have to. Every one of
you, out of here, right now. Ching's going to be kept
quiet, if I have to shoot every damned one of you full
of sedatives! Out, damn it! Not another word!''

He watched, his face like stone, as Teague and Moira
grabbed Fontana around the waist and wrestled her out
of the cabin. She was crying now, tears raining down
her face, her mouth contorted, broken protests still
coming from her lips.

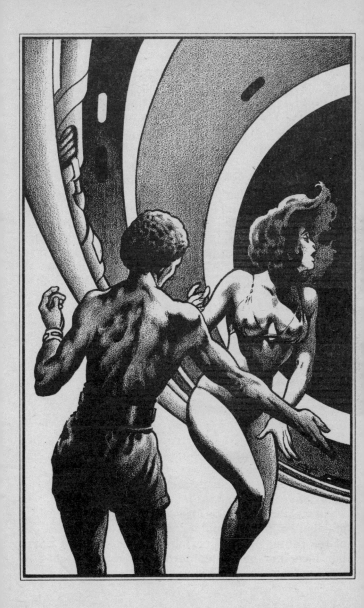

The sphincter locks finally closed behind them; Ravi, always practical, had caught up the full trays of food and taken them along. Peake let himself collapse into his seat, staring at Ching's pale motionless face. After a moment he got up again, got himself a hot caffeine drink from the console and sat down, sipping it, beside Ching.

That was the textbook talking. Suppose Fontana was right, after all? Isn't all this a fairly futile gesture? Should I accept what Fontana said, that we're all dead, and just let Ching die in peace? His face taut, reaching for the almost indefinable pulse, he told himself that the choice might not lie in his hands at all.

CHAPTER TWELVE

Teague thrust Fontana, still struggling, into her cubicle. He said dryly, "Get that hypo ready, Moira."

Fontana had fallen heavily to the floor. She stirred slightly, sat up. Her voice was very calm.

"I don't need it, Teague. I won't make any more trouble, I promise you."

Teague hesitated. Then he said in a hard voice, "We have trouble enough with Ching. I think we should knock you out and make sure you won't give us any more problems."

"No," Fontana said, and Moira interrupted him.

"She's right, Teague. Peake said himself that she's the only one qualified to help him if he needs help. She can't help him if she's doped up. Fontana, do you want me to stay with you? Do you need someone to talk to?"

"No. Really. But I think I — I do need to be alone a while."

Teague still hesitated, but finally he put the hypo away. He said, "All right. But don't let yourself get into that state again. If you need somebody, just yell. One of us will be here." Roughly, he put his arms around her and hugged her hard. "Look, don't worry about it. Peake understands how upset we all are over this. Try and eat something, Fontana."

"All right. Leave me the tray," Fontana said, and when the cubicle door had closed behind them, she sighed, reached for the tray and put a forkful of food — cold now — into her mouth.

In spite of her agitation, she felt deeply moved. In the midst of his own agitation over Ching, he had taken the time to try and comfort her. Yes, he had mistaken the source of her distress, but she felt warmed by his concern.

Yet, after all, why should he not be concerned? They had been friends since the age of five, had briefly been lovers. Teague was not the kind of person to desert an old lover simply because he loved someone else.

They are all my friends, she thought, *I owe it to them to die with as much dignity as they do, and not make it harder for us all to die.*

And then — it was like a blinding light — she thought, *But we are all going to die sometime anyhow. And people have always died. More stupidly than this, more uselessly than this. Before there were spaceships or Academies, there was always the prowling sabre-tooth tiger outside the cave. The very act of being born presupposes death.*

She still felt all the unexpressed rage against the Academy, that could use them this way and fling them out into space like spores of their dying planet. For the planet was dying, or they would not have needed the Academy at all. All of them, all of the students in the Academy, had been exempted for twelve years from all of humanity's lesser and grosser problems, pampered, protected, made into the cream of the cream of the cream of the human race; and we do not suffer from wars, or from famines, or from politics, or from energy shortages, the struggle to survive, family crises, or social upheavals. None of us has ever had any of mankind's lesser problems; because we were being saved for the greatest of their major ones; the very survival of the human race itself. And we cannot expect to live forever in the pampered womb of the Academy. We are struggling with the pains of birth, that is all. And the first of the pains of birth, the first problem of those driven out of our Eden, is the problem of death. *I had never come face to face with death before; that is all. I had never known that one day I must certainly die.*

But there is no need to die before we must, she thought. *And part of my own struggle to live is to help Ching live; and so I must really be ready to assist Peake at whatever he has to do.*

Firmly she sat up, put her fork into the cold and unappetizing food, and began, steadily, to eat it. Afterward she would go and shower and rest and be ready for Peake when — or if — he needed her.

She could even tolerate not knowing whether it would be *when,* or *if.* Humanity had always lived with uncertainties like that. She had simply been exempted from them a little longer than most people, that was all. But someday even the most protected children had to grow up.

Teague turned away from Fontana's door, and shoved his way, not into his own cubicle, but into Ching's deserted one. It was the only way in which he could be close to her. There was the bunk, the safety net still hanging loose from one edge; the net behind which, clipped together, they had made love. It seemed that he could almost feel her delicate body against his, the feel of her small breasts in his hands. He had said something about the perfection of her body, and with that curious mixture of sophistication and naïveté, she had

laughed and said she couldn't claim any credit for it,
it was all due to genetic tinkering anyway, but she was
grateful she had been given that kind of perfection; at
least she wasn't frigid or anything imperfect like that!
They had laughed over that as if it were really funny.

Teague felt as if he would weep again, that guilt
would destroy him. His injured hand throbbed, and he
almost welcomed evidence of sharing her suffering. If
he had not badgered her about her fear of free-fall, if
he had not urged her, she would not have felt so com-
pelled to overcome it, would not have been led into
those damnable, execrable, experiments in the gym.

*She trusted me, she trusted me, she said she knew
I would never let her get hurt . . . .*

Forcibly wrenching his mind away from guilt, he sat
down and ate his tray of cold food. Then, because
Teague was the kind of person who would always take
refuge in action when he was troubled, he busied himself around the cubicle, taking some discarded disposable clothes out to the disposer chute with his tray and
eating utensils, returning to straighten away the mild
disorder of the room. Lying on the small desk-shelf,
meticulously clipped down for safety in free-fall, was
some music which Ching had been reading or studying;
a copy of the *Ave Verum* they had been singing, and,
beneath it, a few lines hand-scribbled, not a neat computer printout. Blinking, Teague recognized the page
of his string quartet that he had crumpled and been
ready to put into the disposer.

It seemed so meaningless now, small and pointless,
when he had been so proud of it. It wasn't music, not
in the sense that Bach was music, it wasn't important
with Ching lying near death, perhaps already dead —
no, Teague clung to the knowledge that Peake would
tell him if there had been any serious change.

He stared at the melody line, hearing it sung in Ching's small sweet voice. She had treasured it, then, she had kept it here so that he would not, in a fit of depression, destroy it.

And suddenly Teague felt the weight of guilt slip from his heart. He had not forced Ching to try the experiment which had led to her accident; she had been eager to be free of the paralyzing fear and incapacity, eager to function in free-fall as well as he did, and the others. It was part of her desire to do everything she did as well as it could possibly be done, part of the character which had made her a computer expert. His guilt was pointless. In the face of the death which might face them all if Ching did not recover, everything was pointless, perhaps.

And yet he looked at his quartet with new, cherishing eyes. Ching had thought it good, worth preserving. Perhaps the quartet was pointless, too, as pointless as his guilt.

But it is as important, and as unimportant, as anything else. And as he smoothed out the sheets, he drew a stylus from his pocket and corrected a minor flaw in the music. He saw that Ching had pencilled in another small correction. And he knew that if they lived through another day, and Ching did not die, he would show the quartet to Peake, who was undeniably the best musician among them, and ask for his opinion and his help. And some day, if they lived, all of them would play it together. That day might never come, but he was going to prepare for it, anyhow.

He curled up his big body into the bunk where he and Ching had made love, and began to scribble on the music paper. He would finish it, for Ching, and for their love, and for himself. And for all of them. Because, if he was important to them, his music was important too, the best of himself to be shared with them all.

Moira found that she was not hungry; but with the discipline of years, she forced herself to eat. Ravi had chosen foods for her that he knew she liked, and she spared him a grateful thought.

She thought how wretchedly ironic it was that Ching, the most perfect among them, the G-N, the self-sufficient, should be the one to fail them.

If she dies, she thought, and quailed from the thought. She was surprised at her own reaction. As recently as the day before they left Earth, she would have thought Ching was the one who would be most readily expendable, the G-N, the one nobody really liked. She herself had admired Ching, but never really liked her; now she faced the fact that she had envied Ching. Envied her her sharp intelligence, the special High-IQ genes of the G-N; and even more, envied her the perfect self-sufficiency. Envied that Ching had not seemed to need men, whereas she herself, Moira, had reached out, always, for approval, wanting to see herself mirrored in other eyes. Men's eyes. Feeling isolated by the Wild Talent, the ESP which had made her feel like a freak, she had turned to sex as some people turn to art, or music, or other forms of self-expression; she had enjoyed the appreciation men gave her body, enjoyed reducing the proudest men to her physical slaves. Yet, she realized miserably, although she had given her body to many men, she had never been able to give to any man the happiness she had seen in Teague's face when Ching snuggled on his lap in the music room.

And now Ching was dying, and Teague had probably got it into his head that it was his fault. *Damn it, no, it wasn't his fault, it was the fault of the damned DeMags;* and, she thought, *my fault too. I'm supposed to be so good with machinery, and I couldn't even find it. And I didn't even trust my ESP enough to tell everybody in no uncertain terms: Stay out of the gym — the trouble isn't over yet.*

Why, she wondered, had she not warned anyone?

And then, humiliated, she knew. If she had demanded, stormed, said that her ESP was giving her severe warnings of more trouble, she would have had to admit that she was a freak, different, not the happy, sexy, carefree Moira they all liked and admired. She would have had, for once, to admit her own difference, her own isolation, that she was not perfectly independent and self-sufficient after all, but a cringing child in the grip of something she, for all her intelligence and all her talent, could not understand.

I was willing to let somebody be killed, rather than admit I was afraid of my own ESP! If Ching dies, how can I ever live with that?

And here I am again, thinking only of myself and not of Ching!

She realized that she had gone to all kinds of lengths to avoid admitting this to herself. She had tried to validate herself by making Ravi her slave, then showing her power over him by rejecting his love. And, staring at the floor, she knew that this, at least, she had the power to put right even if they all died.

If I could offer myself to Peake, who doesn't want me, I can offer myself to Ravi, who wants me in a way that frightens me to think about. I can't do anything to help Ching, just now. I couldn't do anything for Peake except make him uncomfortable; and if I go to Teague he would think, and quite rightly too, that I was trying to take a mean advantage of Ching while she's hurt. The one person I can make happier just now is Ravi.

She put her plate in the disposer and stole quietly toward Ravi's door.

Ravi had turned the DeMags down as low as he could, and curled up cross-legged, in midair, letting his mind go free in meditation. Yet it stayed fiercely locked to his body, without the reassuring freedom of the meditative state.

It was likely, he thought, that they were all going to die. It did not seem to matter. But he felt sick with regret at the waste. So much they might have done. The whole Cosmos waiting out there to be seen and explored, and they would die before they even left the Solar System.

But it seemed that as he floated there, he was a part of the whole Ship, of the whole crew, suffering Peake's shaken lack of confidence, Fontana's surging terror of death, Teague's guilt . . . it even seemed that he shared Ching's lifelessness. He wished fiercely that he had been taught to pray. *There is no human help for this kind of crisis. Therefore we need God.*

And then he wondered, sharply; wasn't it demeaning God, to call on the forces of the Deity for help in purely mundane problems? If God was ineffable, he could not be a kind of super-Mommy, conforting cries and tears and fears. God, if there was a God at all, and Ravi knew he could not admit any such possibility, God had to be something above and beyond all human problems, something not to be questioned about Its divine ways, but accepted, endured, *shared*. God was all of them together, the crew, the Ship, the stars, everything. And how did he dare to think that he alone suffered for some spiritual awareness? It was the same problem every one of them had; how to deal with the terrifying fact that every human being, every atom of material matter, is forever alone, shut up inside the confines of his own thought processes. Everyone needed that awareness of NOT being alone, and when for a moment they were conscious of the truth, that every atom in the great universe needed every other atom, not to DO anything, but simply to BE, then they had realized God. No matter what they called it.

And then he raised his eyes and found that God, whom for the moment he knew in Moira, was beside him, tears raining down her face, holding out her arms.

"Oh, Ravi, Ravi, I need you, I love you so," she whispered, and Ravi knew in that instant he too was God for her.

Peake consulted the chronometer for, it seemed, the fifth or sixth time in an hour. He bent to check Ching's vital signs again; pinched a fold of muscle on her upper arm, brutally. The response was fainter this time, none of the sharp flinching she had shown at first. There was no point putting it off. She was worse. Her response to painful stimuli was diminishing; the last real sign of brain activity. She breathed, her heart beat, her blood moved and was deoxygenated and reoxygenated in her veins, the superb physical organism was there. But where was the real Ching?

He was alone, on this Ship, alone with a crew of hostile strangers, and at this moment they needed him, he was the only one who might be able to save Ching. And to save Ching was to save them all, for Ching was their one hope of repairing the computer, and with it the faulty DeMag units, the problems with navigation, the Ship itself.

So he had no choice but to operate. The question he had asked himself before came back now, with sickening force.

If it had been Jimson, could I have done it? Will I be less squeamish because it is Ching?

And suddenly, touching Ching's cold foot with careful surgeon's fingers, he knew that the answer was yes. He would have operated on Jimson, if the alternative was death; the reason Jimson was not on their crew was because the powers of the Academy had known that Jimson, buried in self-distrust of the thing he had become, would not have been willing to do the same for him.

He had never been alone. Or rather, all during the years with Jimson he had been alone without knowing it; and now he would never be alone again. He had not a single lover, but five of them. It did not matter whether or not he ever managed to bring himself to have sex with any or all of them, though he supposed that some day, now that he was aware of how deeply he was bound to them, that would happen too, in the proper time. But when and if it did, that was irrelevant. The important thing was that for now it was his responsibility to do the best he could for Ching, and for them all. There was no room for a consensus decision now; he could not refuse now to take that responsibility upon himself.

He touched a button to the intercom.

"Fontana and Teague," he said into it, "I need you here. Ching isn't responding, and we need to decide what to do."

CHAPTER THIRTEEN

"Moira," he said, in surprise, "I didn't call you. It's going to be hard enough, operating, in this crowded space, with an unskilled surgical team. There's nothing you can do to help —"

"No, you need me," Moira said quietly. "You need me more than you need Fontana, or Teague. You said you had no X-ray on board. And I know enough anatomy to know what your problem is — the body is only a machine, after all. You're not sure whether Ching has a fracture or not, or whether it's bleeding inside the skull and pressure building up. But I have ESP, Peake. I can find out whether or not the bone is broken, or where the bleeding is."

He looked at her in amazement; he had never thought of this. There had been a tacit agreement among them all not to talk about Moira's ESP, to treat it, not as an asset, but as an odd and humiliating handicap she had to overcome. And yet, looking into her calm green eyes, he knew that she promised no more than she could do.

His lips twitched. "All right," he said, "I can use all the help I can get. Fontana, you'll have to assist; go and scrub up. Teague, can you handle anesthesia? It's sort of an ultimate Life Support; not that she's going to need any anesthesia, except for a little novocaine in the skull, but you ought to stand by. Moira —" he looked down at her, then shook his head. There was nothing he could say in return for this enormous breakthrough, which, if it worked, would certainly mean the difference between life and death for Ching, perhaps for all of them.

"Stay with Ching while I go and get everything ready."

"Do you need her head shaved, Peake?"

"Half," he said, his dark pink-lined finger pointing to the temple, describing a line across Ching's skull. "And rinse with antiseptic solution; Fontana will show you what to do."

Scrubbing for the operation, holding his long muscular hands under the sterilizing light, he found himself in sudden panic. But he took a deep breath, as he had been trained to do, and reminded himself that he really had no choice. Life and death didn't leave anyone much choice.

Ching had been shaved, her head painted with the pinkish antiseptic solution; she looked small, unfamiliar, vulnerable, not quite human. There was no need for anesthesia; nature had done that, the deep coma where she lay. Peake glanced around at the small array of surgical instruments. Fontana had done well.

"Well," he said grimly, "let's get on with it. I hope you know how to use electrocoagulation, Fontana; any opening in the skull means a hell of a lot of blood. Do the best you can to keep the field clear — you *have* assisted before, haven't you?"

She laughed, a small mirthless sound. "I held the retractors once for a normal Caesarian section. And I circumcised a newborn baby. Which is the total sum of my surgical experience. But I can use the aspirators, and I did work with electrocoagulation in the medical laboratory."

Peake thought, *it's worse than I thought. We don't just need luck, we need a bloody damned miracle!* But he said, "Do the best you can."

And as if reading his mind, Ravi said softly, "Remember those Egyptian mummies and the trepan holes in their skulls, Peake. If they could handle it *then*, it ought to be easy enough for you."

Peake said, "Thanks." He gestured to Moira. "If you can tell what —"

She gestured, laying her fingertips close to Ching's skull without touching it. She said, almost in a whisper, "I *know* this, Peake. There's no bone broken there, not even a crack in the skull. It's a — a clot right underneath the bone — does that make any sense at all?"

"Damn right," Peake said. His trained mind remarked, *subdural hematoma. I thought so.* He picked up the small, circular ring saw, tested it for an instant, buzzing, and laid it against the skull to begin the first touch into the bone.

Moira, watching Fontana's hands doing things to clear the gush of blood, wondered how it was that somehow she could see the inside of Ching's skull as readily as the outside, *see* the small, heavy clot of blood. She held a sterile cloth ready, with curiosity and a touch of horror, to receive the small plug of bone. Peake's hands were probing, delicately.

"Got the bastard," he said, holding it up with some small instrument. Moira did not need to look at the blood clot. She had seen it before.

From the table below them a blurry voice spoke.

"What are you — what are you doing with my head? I can't move, I can't see — " and a fretful pulling at the restraining straps.

"It's all right," Teague said, quickly alert. "Peake's just bandaging you up now, you're all right. You can't see because there's a towel over your eyes."

"Oh." The fretful voice subsided, and Peake let his
breath go. He had seen this before; the sudden miracle,
the dead speaking from the tomb. Now that it was over,
he knew that he had been clenched against disaster,
another DeMag failure — what would have happened
if the gravity suddenly disappeared at the moment he
was making the first incision, would the scalpel have
slipped into the brain? Maybe someday there would be
a medical specialty, Free-fall surgery; Peake fervently
hoped he would never find out.

"My head aches a little. What happened?" Ching
murmured in that plaintive, fretful voice.

"You fell. Now lie perfectly still, Ching, it's all right,"
Peake said, in a stern commanding tone, and she was
quiet. He knew that the layer where he was working
was insensitive to pain in the ordinary sense, but the
exposed brain tissue could give rise to irritability.

"Do I have to have my hands tied? I won't move,"
she murmured.

"Sssh, darling, it's all right," Teague soothed, holding her hands, and she subsided. Later, when Peake
was suturing the skull, which really hurt her, she began
to cry softly, but she did not complain; and after a little,
exhausted, she fell asleep before he finished. Normal
sleep, this time; Peake, checking her reflexes as he
transferred her to the stretcher again, realized that she
would sleep, and wake without any memory of the
operation at all. She would have a small scar, and with
luck her hair would grow right back over it. Peake left
Fontana to clear away the operating area — Ravi came
to help, since he had not done anything — and Teague
to stay close to Ching in case she woke and wanted
him, and went to dial himself a very stiff drink from
the console. Medicinal, he told himself firmly, as he

settled down to enjoy it. His chair was next to the bin where Fontana's electronic keyboard was stored, and he found himself thinking of the Schubert *Nocturne* he and Jimson had played at the final concert. He thought of the lovely plaintive melody without bitterness. He and Fontana would play it, when Ching was well enough that they could all make music again.

Moira came to help Ravi put the soiled cloths into the disposer.

She said, "You know, all the time I was watching Peake operate, I was wondering. I should have been able to see inside the DeMags and find the flaw in the controls, just as I saw inside Ching's skull. I've got a lot of exploring to do, to find out what my ESP is really good for."

Ravi smiled at her. "Maybe we can use it to get us back on course again, my darling."

"Nothing's impossible," she said softly, pressing close to him.

And Survey Ship 103 moved past the orbit of Pluto, out into the unknown.